ORANGES ARE NOT THE ONLY FRUIT

ALSO BY JEANETTE WINTERSON

Fiction

The Passion

Sexing the Cherry

Written on the Body

Art & Lies

Gut Symmetries

The World and Other Places

The Powerbook

Lighthousekeeping

Weight

The Stone Gods

Non-Fiction

Art Objects

Why Be Happy When You Could Be Normal?

Comic Book

Boating for Beginners

Children's Books

Tanglewreck

The King of Capri

The Battle of the Sun

The Lion, the Unicorn and Me

Screenplays

Oranges are not the Only Fruit (BBC TV)

Ingenious (BBC TV)

JEANETTE WINTERSON

Oranges Are Not the Only Fruit

VINTAGE BOOKS

London

Published by Vintage 2014

4

Copyright © Jeanette Winterson 1985
Introduction copyright © Jeanette Winterson 2014

Jeanette Winterson has asserted her right to be identified as the
author of this work under the Copyright, Designs and Patents Act
1988

First published in Great Britain in 1985 by Pandora Press
First published by Vintage in 1991

Random House, 20 Vauxhall Bridge Road,
London SW1V 2SA
www.vintage-books.co.uk

Addresses for companies within The Random House Group Limited
can be found at: www.randomhouse.co.uk/offices.htm

The Random House Group Limited Reg. No. 954009

A CIP catalogue record for this book
is available from the British Library

ISBN 9780099598183

Penguin Random House is committed to a sustainable future for
our business, our readers and our planet. This book is made from
Forest Stewardship Council® certified paper.

Printed and bound in Great Britain by Clays Ltd, St Ives plc

TO PHILIPPA BREWSTER WHO WAS THE BEGINNING

'When thick rinds are used the top must be thoroughly skimmed, or a scum will form marring the final appearance.'

From *The Making of Marmalade* by Mrs Beeton

'Oranges are not the only fruit'

Nell Gwynn

CONTENTS

INTRODUCTION

When *Oranges Are Not The Only Fruit* was first published in 1985 it was often stocked in the cookbooks section with the marmalade manuals.

The title is attributed by me to Nell Gwynn, raunchy mistress of Charles 1st, possessor of fabulous breasts, and famously painted as an orange-seller. I thought she might have said oranges are not the only fruit, but she didn't. What is the point of being a fiction writer if you can't make things up?

Oranges is autobiographical in so much as I used my own life as the base for a story. There's nothing unusual about that. The trick is to turn your own life into something that has meaning for people whose experience is nothing like your own. Write what you know is reasonable advice. Read what you don't know is better advice.

Reading is an adventure. Adventures are about the unknown. When I started to read seriously I was excited and comforted all at the same time. Literature is a mix of unfamiliarity and recognition. The situation can take us anywhere – across time and space, the globe, through the lives of people who can never be like us – into the heart of anguish we have never felt – crimes we could not commit.

Yet as we travel deeper into the strange world of

the story, the feeling we get is of being understood – which is odd when you think about it, because at school learning is based on whether or not we understand what we are reading. In fact it is the story (or the poem) that is understanding us.

Books read us back to ourselves.

And one of the things the story teaches us is this: Read yourself as a fiction as well as a fact.

When I was growing up poor in a poor place with a pair of Pentecostal parents who were waiting for Jesus to return and roll up time and space like a scroll, I never thought my life was narrow or my chances bleak. I thought I was Heathcliff, Huck Finn, Hotspur, Aladdin, the Big Bad Wolf. The Fish with a Golden Ring.

And later, when I had left home at sixteen and was living in a Mini, I had my favourite books stashed in the boot and whenever I could be in the library, I was there. This wasn't a fantasy world or escapism – though it was an escape; it was the hidden door in the blank wall. Open it.

I opened the book and went through.

The escape into another story reminds us that we too are another story. Not caught, not confined, not pre-destined, not only one gender or passion. Learning to read yourself as a fiction as well as a fact is liberating – it is the difference between energy and mass. Mass is the beloved object – the world we can touch and feel – but mass is also the dead weight in ourselves and others.

Shifting the dead weight takes energy but at its atomic core the dead weight *is* energy. Transforming mass into energy, energy into mass is what creative work is about.

An idea becomes embodied. A tragedy is released.

Oranges works with fairy stories and in particular the Grail Legend because I am drawn to this fundamental truth about how situations can be transformed – and why they are not – which is what tragedy is all about. The Grail Legend ends badly but not hopelessly. And I suppose that even tragedy as its most bleak contains an energetic core of hope, because as spectators we realise that nothing has to end the way it does. That it does end the way it does – and often badly – need not be the final answer.

Even those words, 'final' and 'answer' are faulty. The human process is continuous. And dimensional. Answers happen as movement, not stasis.

And doesn't every fairy tale begin with a problem that is stuck?

The Kingdom is sick. The King has no heir. The Princess is lost. The Dragon is eating everyone. The Hero is dead. And so on

I was born without prospects. So I wrote myself the world I wanted to find. There is a line in *Oranges*: 'What I want does exist if I dare to find it.'

I was 23. Taking risks is essential. Any fairy tale will tell you that.

People often ask me why I have used my own name in *Oranges* when it is a novel.

It wasn't because I couldn't think of another name or because I was signalling that *Oranges* is a memoir; it was about self-invention.

I wanted to use myself as a fictional character – an expanded 'I'.

xiv   ORANGES ARE NOT THE ONLY FRUIT

Adopted children are self-invented because we have to be; we arrive with the first pages of our story torn out. Writers are self-inventors too – we have to be – so in my case a capacity or a cast of character, (yes, that becomes a cast of characters – the multiple self of the writer) is strongly in the ascendant. Given what I am, I don't see what else I could be, but a fictioneer.

I never wanted a literal reading of *Oranges*. If I call myself Jeanette why must I be writing an autobiography? Henry Miller calls his hero Henry. Paul Auster and Milan Kundra call themselves by name in some of their work. So does Philip Roth. This is understood by critics as playful meta-fiction. For a woman it is assumed to be confessional. Is this assumption about gender? Something to do with creative authority? Why shouldn't a woman be her own experiment?

Oranges Are Not The Only Fruit is a novel.

I suppose I have, in a way, gone on using my own name in everything I have written because I prefer to write in the First Person. I am I and I am Not-I.

Understood?

Part fact part fiction is what life is.

When *Oranges* got out of the Preserves section it went into the Gay/Lesbian section – either because I am gay or because being gay is part of what the book is about. That is fine by me though why are we so busy with the labels? *Oranges* is for anybody and everybody – all of my books are for anybody and everybody.

After a while, and having become a modern classic, *Oranges* went into the Literature section too. Had I been a straight white male the confidence of the writing and the experiment with form and material, would have put it there to begin with – well maybe with a detour round Jam.

Thankfully the old assumptions are slowly being killed off. I am glad that *Oranges* is one of the murder weapons.

27 years after I wrote *Oranges* I came back to some of that material because I wanted to write a memoir. The trigger was the discovery of surprising information about my biological mother. As I tried to find her like a detective story I started to think again about Wintersonworld. Out of that collision of past and present I wrote *Why Be Happy When You Could Be Normal?*

That title was one of Mrs Winterson's best lines. She was a violent philosopher.

But let's think for a minute about Memory versus Invention.

Memory is not a filing system, or even a reconstruction; it is a re-creation. We remember the same thing differently at different times not because we are unreliable but because the past is not fixed. Even a simple memory is a cluster of experience where some things are vivid and some things obscured. As we develop and change so do our memories. Freud, one of the grand masters of narrative, understood that we can change the story because we are the story.

We keep telling ourselves to ourselves – telling

ourselves to others – and sometimes one single detail rediscovered or removed is enough to change the balance of what we know.

There has been a lot of discussion about False Memory Syndrome. Sometimes what we remember is a cover-story for what we will not allow ourselves to remember. It's complicated.

Truth is what is left out as well as what is included. As a writer you work constantly to select and reject material. Memory works in the same way but with a different purpose. We are time travellers in our own lives.

When I look back what do I see? A long stretchy street with a town at the bottom and a hill at the top. Myself, walking. Leaving stories as markers as I go. I am trying to make sense of being human. So are you. The story is waiting for you when you pass this way.

GENESIS

LIKE MOST PEOPLE I lived for a long time with my mother and father. My father liked to watch the wrestling, my mother liked to wrestle; it didn't matter what. She was in the white corner and that was that.

She hung out the largest sheets on the windiest days. She *wanted* the Mormons to knock on the door. At election time in a Labour mill town she put a picture of the Conservative candidate in the window.

She had never heard of mixed feelings. There were friends and there were enemies.

Enemies were: The Devil (in his many forms)
Next Door
Sex (in its many forms)
Slugs
Friends were: God
Our dog
Auntie Madge
The Novels of Charlotte Brontë
Slug pellets

and me, at first, I had been brought in to join her in a tag match against the Rest of the World. She had a mysterious attitude towards the begetting of children; it wasn't that she couldn't do it, more that she didn't want to do it. She was very bitter about the Virgin Mary getting there first. So she did the next best thing and arranged for a foundling. That was me.

I cannot recall a time when I did not know that I was special. We had no Wise Men because she didn't believe there were any wise men, but we had sheep. One of my earliest memories is me sitting on a sheep at Easter while she told me the story of the Sacrificial Lamb. We had it on Sundays with potato.

Sunday was the Lord's day, the most vigorous day of the whole week; we had a radiogram at home with an imposing mahogany front and a fat Bakelite knob to twiddle for the stations. Usually we listened to the Light Programme, but on Sundays always the World Service, so that my mother could record the progress of our missionaries. Our Missionary Map was very fine. On the front were all the countries and on the back a number chart that told you about Tribes and their Peculiarities. My favourite was Number 16, *The Buzule of Carpathian*. They believed that if a mouse found your hair clippings and built a nest with them you got a headache. If the nest was big enough, you might go mad. As far as I knew no missionary had yet visited them.

My mother got up early on Sundays and allowed no one into the parlour until ten o'clock. It was her place of prayer and meditation. She always prayed standing up, because of her knees, just as Bonaparte always gave orders from his horse, because of his size. I do think that the relationship my mother enjoyed with God had a lot to do with positioning. She was Old Testament through and through. Not for her the meek and paschal Lamb, she was out there, up front with the prophets, and much given to sulking under trees when the appropriate destruction didn't materialise. Quite often it did, her will or the Lord's I can't say.

She always prayed in exactly the same way. First of all she thanked God that she had lived to see another day, and then she thanked God for sparing the world another day. Then she spoke of her enemies, which was the nearest thing she had to a catechism.

As soon as 'Vengeance is mine saith the Lord' boomed through the wall into the kitchen, I put the kettle on. The time it took to boil the water and brew the tea was just about the length of her final item, the sick list. She was very regular. I put the milk in, in she came, and taking a great gulp of tea said one of three things.

'The Lord is good' (steely-eyed into the back yard).

'What sort of tea is this?' (steely-eyed at me).

'Who was the oldest man in the Bible?'

No. 3 of course, had a number of variations, but it was always a Bible quiz question. We had a lot of Bible quizzes at church and my mother liked me to win. If I knew the answer she asked me another, if I didn't she got cross, but luckily not for long, because we had to listen to the World Service. It was always the same; we sat down on either side of the radiogram, she with her tea, me with a pad and pencil; in front of us, the Missionary Map. The faraway voice in the middle of the set gave news of activities, converts and problems. At the end there was an appeal for YOUR PRAYERS. I had to write it all down so that my mother could deliver her church report that night. She was the Missionary Secretary. The Missionary Report was a great trial to me because our mid-day meal depended upon it. If it went well, no deaths and lots of converts, my mother cooked a joint. If the Godless had proved not only stubborn, but murderous, my mother spent the rest of the morning listening to the Jim Reeves Devotional Selection, and we had to have boiled eggs and toast soldiers. Her husband was an easy-going man, but I knew it depressed him. He would have cooked it himself but for my mother's complete conviction that she was the only person in our house who would tell a saucepan from a piano. She was wrong, as far as we were concerned, but right as far as she was concerned, and really, that's what mattered.

Somehow we got through those mornings, and in the afternoon she and I took the dog for a walk, while my father cleaned all the shoes. 'You can tell someone by their shoes,' my mother said. 'Look at Next Door.'

'Drink,' said my mother grimly as we stepped out past their house. 'That's why they buy everything from Maxi Ball's Catalogue Seconds. The Devil himself is a drunk' (sometimes my mother invented theology).

Maxi Ball owned a warehouse, his clothes were cheap but they didn't last, and they smelt of industrial glue. The desperate, the careless, the poorest, vied with one another on a Saturday morning to pick up what they could, and haggle over the price. My mother would rather not eat than be seen at Maxi Ball's. She had filled me with a horror of the place. Since so many people we knew went there, it was hardly fair of her but she never was particularly fair; she loved and she hated, and she hated Maxi Ball. Once, in winter, she had been forced to go there to buy a corset and in the middle of communion, that very Sunday, a piece of whalebone slipped out and stabbed her right in the stomach. There was nothing she could do for an hour. When we got home she tore up the corset and used the whalebone as supports for our geraniums, except for one piece that she gave to me. I still have it, and whenever I'm tempted to cut corners I think about that whalebone and I know better.

My mother and I walked on towards the hill that stood at the top of our street. We lived in a town stolen from the valleys, a huddled place full of chimneys and little shops and back-to-back houses with no gardens. The hills surrounded us, and our own swept out into the Pennines, broken now and again with a farm or a relic from the war. There used to be a lot of old tanks but the council took them away. The town was a fat blot and the streets spread back from it into the green, steadily upwards. Our house was almost at the top of a long, stretchy street. A flagged street with a cobbly road. When you climb to the top of the hill and look down you can see everything, just like Jesus on the pinnacle except it's not very tempting. Over to the right was the viaduct and behind the viaduct Ellison's tenement, where we had the fair once a year. I was allowed to go there on condition I brought back a tub of black peas for my mother. Black peas look like rabbit droppings and they come in a thin gravy made of stock and gypsy mush. They taste wonderful. The gypsies made a mess and stayed up all night and my mother called them fornicators but on the whole we got on very well. They turned a blind eye to toffee apples going missing, and sometimes, if it was quiet and you didn't have enough money, they still let you have a ride on the dodgems. We used to have fights round the caravans, the ones like me, from the street, against the posh ones from the Avenue. The posh ones went to Brownies and didn't stay for school dinners.

Once, when I was collecting the black peas, about to go home, the old woman got hold of my hand. I thought she was going to bite me. She looked at my palm and laughed a bit. 'You'll never marry,' she said, 'not you, and you'll never be still.' She didn't take any money for the peas, and she told me to run home fast. I ran and ran, trying to understand what she meant. I hadn't thought about getting married anyway. There were two women I knew who didn't have any husbands at all; they were old though, as old as my mother. They ran the paper shop and sometimes, on a Wednesday, they gave me a banana bar with my comic. I liked them a lot, and talked about them a lot to my mother. One day they asked me if I'd like to go to the seaside with them. I ran home, gabbled it out, and was busy emptying my money box to buy a new spade, when my mother said firmly and forever, no. I couldn't understand why not, and she wouldn't explain. She didn't even let me go back to say I couldn't. Then she cancelled my comic and told me to collect it from another shop, further away. I was sorry about that. I never got a banana bar from Grimsby's. A couple of weeks later I heard her telling Mrs White about it. She said they dealt in unnatural passions. I thought she meant they put chemicals in their sweets.

My mother and I climbed until the town fell away and we reached the memorial stone at the very top.

The wind was always strong so that my mother had to wear extra hat pins. Usually she wore a headscarf, but not on Sunday. We sat on the stone's base and she thanked the Lord we had managed the ascent. Then she extemporised on the nature of the world, the folly of its peoples, and the wrath of God inevitable. After that she told me a story about a brave person who had despised the fruits of the flesh and worked for the Lord instead . . .

There was the story of the 'converted sweep', a filthy degenerate, given to drunkenness and vice, who suddenly found the Lord whilst scraping the insides of a flue. He remained in the flue in a state of rapture for so long that his friends thought he was unconscious. After a great deal of difficulty they persuaded him to come out; his face, they declared, though hardly visible for the grime, shone like an angel's. He started to lead the Sunday School and died some time later, bound for glory. There were many more; I particularly like the 'Hallelujah Giant', a freak of nature, eight feet tall shrunk to six foot three through the prayers of the faithful.

Now and again my mother liked to tell me her own conversion story; it was very romantic. I sometimes think that if Mills and Boon were at all revivalist in their policy my mother would be a star.

One night, by mistake, she had walked into Pastor Spratt's Glory Crusade. It was in a tent on some spare land, and every evening Pastor Spratt spoke of the fate of the damned, and performed healing miracles. He was very impressive. My mother said he looked like Errol Flynn, but holy. A lot of women found the Lord that week. Part of Pastor Spratt's charisma stemmed from his time spent as an advertising manager for Rathbone's Wrought Iron. He knew about bait. 'There is nothing wrong with bait,' he said, when the Chronicle somewhat cynically asked him why he gave pot plants to the newly converted. 'We are commanded to be Fishers of Men.' When my mother heard the call, she was presented with a copy of the Psalms and asked to make her choice between a Christmas Cactus (non-flowering) and a lily of the valley. She had opted for the lily of the valley. When my father went the next night, she told him to be sure and go for the cactus, but by the time he got to the front they had all gone. 'He's not one to push himself,' she often said, and after a little pause, 'Bless him.'

Pastor Spratt came to stay with them for the rest of his time with the Glory Crusade, and it was then that my mother discovered her abiding interest in missionary work. The pastor himself spent most of his time out in the jungle and other hot places converting the Heathen. We have a picture of him surrounded by black men with spears. My mother keeps it by her bed. My mother is very like William Blake; she has visions and dreams and she cannot always distinguish a flea's head from a king. Luckily she can't paint.

She walked out one night and thought of her life and thought of what was possible. She thought of the things she couldn't be. Her uncle had been an actor. 'A very fine Hamlet,' said the *Chronicle*.

But the rags and the ribbons turn to years and then the years are gone. Uncle Will had died a pauper, she was not so young these days and people were not kind. She liked to speak French and to play the piano, but what do these things mean?

★

Once upon a time there was a brilliant and beautiful princess, so sensitive that the death of a moth could distress her for weeks on end. Her family knew of no solution. Advisers wrung their hands, sages shook their heads, brave kings left unsatisfied. So it happened for many years, until one day, out walking in the forest, the princess came to the hut of an old hunchback who knew the secrets of magic. This ancient creature perceived in the princess a woman of great energy and resourcefulness.

'My dear,' she said, 'you are in danger of being burned by your own flame.'

The hunchback told the princess that she was old, and wished to die, but could not because of her many responsibilities. She had in her charge a small village of homely people, to whom she was advisor and friend. Perhaps the princess would like to take over? Her duties would be:

(1) To milk the goats
(2) To educate the people
(3) To compose songs for their festival

To assist her she would have a three-legged stool and all the books belonging to the hunchback. Best of all, the old woman's harmonium, an instrument of great antiquity and four octaves. The princess agreed to stay and forgot all about the palace and the moths. The old woman thanked her, and died at once.

My mother, out walking that night, dreamed a dream and sustained it in daylight. She would get a child, train it, build it, dedicate it to the Lord:

a missionary child,
a servant of God,
a blessing

And so it was that on a particular day, some time later, she followed a star until it came to settle above an orphanage, and in that place was a crib, and in that crib, a child. A child with too much hair.

She said, 'This child is mine from the Lord'.

She took the child away and for seven days and seven nights the child cried out, for fear and not knowing. The mother sang to the child, and stabbed the demons. She understood how jealous the Spirit is of flesh.

Such warm tender flesh.

Her flesh now, sprung from her head.

Her vision.

Not the jolt beneath the hip bone, but water and the word.

She had a way out now, for years and years to come.

We stood on the hill and my mother said, 'This world is full of sin.'

We stood on the hill and my mother said, 'You can change the world.'

When we got home my father was watching television. It was the match between 'Crusher Williams' and one-eyed Jonney Stott. My mother was furious; we always covered up the television on Sundays. We had a DEEDS OF THE OLD TESTAMENT tablecloth, given to us by a man who did house clearances. It was very grand, and we kept it in a special drawer with nothing else but a piece of Tiffany glass and some parchment from Lebanon. I don't know why we kept the parchment. We had thought it was a bit of the Old Testament but it was the lease to a sheep farm. My father hadn't even bothered to fold up the cloth, and I could just see 'Moses Receiving the Ten Commandments' in a heap under the vertical hold. 'There's going to be trouble,' I thought, and announced my intention of going down to the Salvation Army place for a tambourine lesson.

Poor Dad, he was never quite good enough.

That night at church, we had a visiting speaker, Pastor Finch from Stockport. He was an expert in demons, and delivered a terrifying sermon on how easy it is to become demon-possessed. We were all very uneasy afterwards. Mrs White said she thought her next-door neighbours were probably possessed, they had all the signs. Pastor Finch said that the possessed are given to uncontrollable rages, sudden bursts of wild laughter, and are always, always, very cunning. The Devil himself, he reminded us, can come as an angel of light.

After the service we were having a banquet; my mother had made twenty trifles and her usual mound of cheese and onion sandwiches.

'You can always tell a good woman by her sand-wiches,' declared Pastor Finch.

My mother blushed.

Then he turned to me and said, 'How old are you, little girl?'

'Seven,' I replied.

'Ah, seven,' he muttered. 'How blessed, the seven

days of creation, the seven-branched candlestick, the seven seals.'

(Seven seals? I had not yet reached Revelation in my directed reading, and I thought he meant some Old Testament amphibians I had overlooked. I spent weeks trying to find them, in case they came up as a quiz question.)

'Yes,' he went on, 'how blessed,' then his brow clouded. 'But how cursed.' At this word his fist hit the table and catapulted a cheese sandwich into the collection bag; I saw it happen, but I was so distracted I forgot to tell anyone. They found it in there the week after, at the Sisterhood meeting. The whole table had fallen silent, except for Mrs Rothwell who was stone deaf and very hungry.

'The demon can return SEVENFOLD.' His eyes roamed the table. (Scrape, went Mrs Rothwell's spoon.)

'SEVENFOLD.'

('Does anybody want this piece of cake?' asked Mrs Rothwell.)

'The best can become the worst,' – he took me by the hand – 'This innocent child, this bloom of the Covenant.'

'Well, I'll eat it then,' announced Mrs Rothwell.

Pastor Finch glared at her, but he wasn't a man to be put off.

'This little lily could herself be a house of demons.'

'Eh, steady on Roy,' said Mrs Finch anxiously.

'Don't interrupt me Grace,' he said firmly, 'I mean this by way of example only. God has given me an opportunity and what God has given we must not presume to waste.

'It has been known for the most holy men to be

suddenly filled with evil. And how much more a woman, and how much more a child. Parents, watch your children for the signs. Husbands, watch your wives. Blessed be the name of the Lord.'

He let go of my hand, which was now crumpled and soggy.

He wiped his own on his trouser leg.

'You shouldn't tax yourself so, Roy,' said Mrs Finch, 'have some trifle, it's got sherry in it.'

I felt a bit awkward too so I went into the Sunday School Room. There was some Fuzzy Felt to make Bible scenes with, and I was just beginning to enjoy a rewrite of Daniel in the lions' den when Pastor Finch appeared. I put my hands into my pockets and looked at the lino.

'Little girl,' he began, then he caught sight of the Fuzzy Felt.

'What's that?'

'Daniel,' I answered.

'But that's not right,' he said, aghast. 'Don't you know that Daniel escaped? In your picture the lions are swallowing him.'

'I'm sorry,' I replied, putting on my best, blessed face. 'I wanted to do Jonah and the whale, but they don't do whales in Fuzzy Felt. I'm pretending those lions are whales.'

'You said it was Daniel.' He was suspicious.

'I got mixed up.'

He smiled. 'Let's put it right, shall we?' And he carefully rearranged the lions in one corner, and Daniel in the other. 'What about Nebuchadnezzar? Let's do the Astonishment at Dawn scene next.' He started to root through the Fuzzy Felt, looking for a king.

'Hopeless,' I thought, Susan Green was sick on the tableau of the three Wise Men at Christmas, and you only get three kings to a box.

I left him to it. When I came back into the hall somebody asked me if I'd seen Pastor Finch.

'He's in the Sunday School Room playing with the Fuzzy Felt,' I replied.

'Don't be fanciful Jeanette,' said the voice. I looked up. It was Miss Jewsbury; she always talked like that, I think it was because she taught the oboe. It does something to your mouth.

'Time to go home,' said my mother. 'I think you've had enough excitement for one day.'

It's odd, the things other people think are exciting.

We set off, my mother, Alice and May ('Auntie Alice, Auntie May, to you'). I lagged behind, thinking about Pastor Finch and how horrible he was. His teeth stuck out, and his voice was squeaky, even though he tried to make it deep and stern. Poor Mrs Finch. How did she live with him? Then I remembered the gypsy. 'You'll never marry.' That might not be such a bad thing after all. We walked along the Factory Bottoms to get home. The poorest people of all lived there, tied to the mills. There were hundreds of children and scraggy dogs. Next Door used to live down there, right by the glue works, but their cousin or someone had left them a house, next to our house. 'The work of the Devil, if ever I saw it,' said my mother, who always believed these things are sent to try us. I wasn't allowed in the Factory Bottoms on my own, and that night as the rain began, I was sure I knew why. If the demons lived anywhere it was here. We went past the shop that sold flea collars and

poisons. Arkwright's For Vermin it was called; I had
been inside it once, when we had a run of cockroaches. Mrs Arkwright was there cashing up; she
caught sight of May as we went past and shouted at
her to come in. My mother wasn't very pleased, but
muttering something about Jesus associating with tax
collectors and sinners pushed me inside, in front of
them all.

'Where've you been May,' asked Mrs Arkwright,
wiping her hand on a dishcloth, 'not seen hide of you
in a month.'

'I've been in Blackpool.'

'Ho, come in at some money have you?'

'It were at Bingo 'ousie 'ousie three times.'

'No.'

Mrs Arkwright was both admiring and bad-tempered.

The conversation continued like this for some time,
Mrs Arkwright complaining that business was poor,
that she'd have to close the shop, that there was no
money in vermin any more.

'Let's hope we have a hot summer, that'll fetch
them out.'

My mother was visibly distressed.

'Remember that heatwave two years ago? Ooo, I
did some trade then. Cockroaches, hard backs, rats,
you name it, I poisoned it. No, it's not same any more.'

We kept a respectful silence for a moment or two,
then my mother coughed and said we should be
getting along.

'Here, then,' said Mrs Arkwright, 'tek these furt nipper.'

She meant me and, rummaging around somewhere
behind the counter, pulled out a few different-shaped
tins.

'It can keep its marbles and stuff in 'em,' she explained.

'Ta,' I said and smiled.

'Ey, it's all right that one, you knows,' she smiled at me and, wiping her hand firmly on my hand, let us out of the shop.

'Look at these May,' I held them up.

'Auntie May,' snapped my mother.

May examined them with me.

'"Silver fish,"' she read. '"Sprinkle liberally behind sinks, toilets and other damp places." Oh, very nice. What's this one: "Lice, bed bugs, etc. Guaranteed effective or money back."'

Eventually we got home, Goodnight May, Goodnight Alice, God Bless. My father had already gone to bed because he worked early shifts. My mother wouldn't be going to bed for hours.

As long as I have known them, my mother has gone to bed at four, and my father has got up at five. That was nice in a way because it meant I could come down in the middle of the night and not be lonely. Quite often we'd have bacon and eggs and she'd read me a bit of the Bible.

It was in this way that I began my education: she taught me to read from the Book of Deuteronomy, and she told me all about the lives of the saints, how they were really wicked, and given to nameless desires. Not fit for worship; this was yet another heresy of the Catholic Church and I was not be misled by the smooth tongues of priests.

'But I never see any priests.'

'A girl's motto is BE PREPARED.'

I learnt that it rains when clouds collide with a high building, like a steeple, or a cathedral; the impact punctures them, and everybody underneath gets wet. This was why, in the old days, when the only tall buildings were holy, people used to say cleanliness is next to godliness. The more godly your town, the more high buildings you'd have, and the more rain you'd get.

'That's why all these Heathen places are so dry,' explained my mother, then she looked into space, and her pencil quivered. 'Poor Pastor Spratt.'

I discovered that everything in the natural world was a symbol of the Great Struggle between good and evil. 'Consider the mamba,' said my mother. 'Over short distances the mamba can outrun a horse.' And she drew the race on a sheet of paper. She meant that in the short term, evil can triumph, but never for very long. We were very glad, and we sang our favourite hymn, *Yield Not to Temptation*.

I asked my mother to teach me French, but her face clouded over, and she said she couldn't.

'Why not?'

'It was nearly my downfall.'

'What do you mean?' I persisted, whenever I could. But she only shook her head and muttered something about me being too young, that I'd find out all too soon, that it was nasty.

'One day,' she said finally, 'I'll tell you about Pierre,' then she switched on the radio and ignored me for so long that I went back to bed.

Quite often, she'd start to tell me a story and then go on to something else in the middle, so I never found out what happened to the Earthly Paradise when it stopped being off the coast of India, and I was stuck at 'six sevens are forty-two' for almost a week.

'Why don't I go to school?' I asked her. I was curious about school because my mother always called it a Breeding Ground. I didn't know what she meant, but I knew it was a bad thing, like Unnatural Passions. 'They'll lead you astray,' was the only answer I got.

I thought about all this in the toilet. It was outside, and I hated having to go at night because of the spiders that came over from the coal-shed. My dad and me always seemed to be in the toilet, me sitting on my hands and humming, and him standing up, I supposed. My mother got very angry.

'You come on in, it doesn't take that long.'

But it was the only place to go. We all shared the same bedroom, because my mother was building us a bathroom in the back, and eventually, if she got the partition fitted, a little half-room for me. She worked very slowly though, because she said she had a lot on her mind. Sometimes Mrs White came round to help mix the grout, but then they'd both end up listening to Johnny Cash, or writing a new hand-out on Baptism by Total Immersion. She did finish eventually, but not for three years.

Meanwhile, my lessons continued, I learnt about Horticulture and Garden Pests via the slugs and my mother's seed catalogues, and I developed an understanding of Historical Process through the prophecies in the Book of Revelation, and a magazine called *The Plain Truth*, which my mother received each week.

'It's Elijah in our midst again,' she declared.

And so I learned to interpret the signs and wonders that the unbeliever might never understand.

'You'll need to when you're out there on the mission field,' she reminded me.

Then, one morning, when we had got up early to listen to Ivan Popov from behind the Iron Curtain, a fat brown envelope plopped through the letter box. My mother thought it was letters of thanks from those who had attended our Healing of the Sick crusade in the town hall. She ripped it open, then her face fell.

'What is it?' I asked her.

'It's about you.'

'What about me?'

'I have to send you to school.'

I whizzed into the toilet and sat on my hands; the Breeding Ground at last.

EXODUS

'WHY DO YOU want me to go?' I asked her the night before.

'Because if you don't go, I'll have to go to prison.' She picked up the knife. 'How many slices do you want?'

'Two,' I said. 'What's going in them?'

'Potted beef, and be thankful.'

'But if you go to prison you'll get out again. St Paul was always going to prison.'

'I know that' (she cut the bread firmly, so that only the tiniest squirt of potted beef oozed out) . . . 'but the neighbours don't. Eat this and be quiet.'

She pushed the plate in front of me. It looked horrible.

'Why can't we have chips?'

'Because I haven't time to make you chips. There's my feet to soak, your vest to iron, and I haven't touched all those requests for prayer. Besides, there's no potatoes.'

I went into the living room, looking for something to do. In the kitchen I heard my mother switch on the radio.

'And now,' said a voice, 'a programme about the family life of snails.'

My mother shrieked.

'Did you hear that?' she demanded, and poked her

head round the kitchen door. 'The family life of snails, it's an Abomination, it's like saying we come from monkeys.'

I thought about it. Mr and Mrs Snail at home on a wet Wednesday night; Mr Snail dozing quietly, Mrs Snail reading a book about difficult children. *'I'm so worried doctor. He's so quiet, won't come out of his shell.'*

'No mum,' I replied, 'it's not like that at all.'

But she wasn't listening. She had gone back into the kitchen, and I could hear her muttering to herself against the static as she fiddled for the World Service. I went after her. 'The Devil's in the world, but not in this house,' she said, and fixed her gaze on the picture of the Lord hung about the oven. It was a watercolour about nine inches square, painted by Pastor Spratt for my mother, before he left with his Glory Crusade for Wigan and Africa.

It was called 'The Lord Feeding the Birds' and my mother put it over the oven because she spent most of her time there, making things for the faithful. It was a bit battered now, and the Lord had a blob of egg on one foot, but we didn't like to touch it in case the paint came off too.

'I've had enough,' she said. 'Go away.'

And she closed the kitchen door again and switched off the radio. I could hear her humming *Glorious Things of Thee are spoken*.

'Well, that's that then,' I thought.

And it was.

The next morning was a hive of activity. My mother dragged me out of bed, shouting that it was half-past seven, that she had had no sleep at all, that my dad had gone to work without his dinner. She poured a scalding kettle of water into the sink.

'Why didn't you go to bed?' I asked her.

'No point if I had to get up with you three hours later.' She shot a jet of cold water into the hot.

'Well you could have had an early night,' I suggested, struggling with my pyjama top. An old woman had made it for me, and made the neck hole the same size as the arm holes, so I always had sore ears. Once I went deaf for three months with my adenoids: no one noticed that either.

I was lying in bed one night, thinking about the glory of the Lord, when it struck me that life had gone very quiet. I had been to church as usual, sung as loudly as ever, but it had seemed for some time that I was the only one making a noise.

I had assumed myself to be in a state of rapture, not uncommon in our church, and later I discovered my mother had assumed the same. When May had asked why I wasn't answering anybody, my mother had said, 'It's the Lord.'

'What's the Lord?' May was confused.

'Working in mysterious ways,' declared my mother, and walked ahead.

So, unknown to me, word spread about our church that I was in a state of rapture, and no one should speak to me.

'Why do you think it's happened?' Mrs White wanted to know.

'Oh, it's not surprising, she's seven you know,' May paused for effect, 'It's a holy number, strange things happen in sevens, look at Elsie Norris.'

★

Elsie Norris, 'Testifying Elsie' as she was called, was a great encouragement to our church. Whenever the pastor asked for a testimony on God's goodness, Elsie leapt to her feet and cried, 'Listen to what the Lord has done for me this week.'

She needed eggs, the Lord had sent them.

She had a bout of colic, the Lord took it away.

She always prayed for two hours a day;

once in the morning at seven a.m.

and once in the evening at seven p.m.

Her hobby was numerology, and she never read the Word without first casting the dice to guide her.

'One dice for the chapter, and one dice for the verse' was her motto.

Someone once asked her what she did for books of the Bible that had more than six chapters.

'I have my ways,' she said stiffly, 'and the Lord has his.'

I liked her a lot because she had interesting things in her house. She had an organ that you had to pedal if you wanted it to make a noise. Whenever I went there she played *Lead Kindly Light*. Her doing the keys, and me doing the pedals because she had asthma. She collected foreign coins and kept them in a glass case that smelled of linseed oil. She said it reminded her of her late husband who had used to play cricket for Lancashire.

'Hard Hand Stan they called him,' she said every time I went to see her. She could never remember what she told people. She could never remember how long she kept her fruit cake. There was a time when I got offered the same piece of cake for five weeks. I was lucky, she never remembered what you said to her either, so every week I made the same excuse.

'Colic,' I said.

'I'll pray for you,' she said.

Best of all, she had a collage of Noah's Ark. It showed the two parent Noah's leaning out looking at the flood, while the other Noah's tried to catch one of the rabbits. But for me, the delight was a detachable chimpanzee, made out of a Brillo pad; at the end of my visit she let me play with it for five minutes. I had all kinds of variations, but usually I drowned it.

One Sunday the pastor told everyone how full of the spirit I was. He talked about me for twenty minutes, and I didn't hear a word; just sat there reading my Bible and thinking what a long book it was. Of course this seeming modesty made them all the more convinced.

I thought no one was talking to me and the others thought I wasn't talking to them. But on the night I realized I couldn't hear anything I went downstairs and wrote on a piece of paper, 'Mother, the world is very quiet.'

My mother nodded and carried on with her book. She had got it in the post that morning from Pastor Spratt. It was a description of missionary life called *Other Continents Know Him Too*.

I couldn't attract her attention, so I took an orange and went back to bed. I had to find out for myself.

Someone had given me a recorder and a tune book for my birthday, so I propped myself up against the pillows and piped out a couple of verses of *Auld Lang Syne*.

I could see my fingers moving, but there was no sound.

I tried *Little Brown Jug*.

Nothing.

In despair I started to beat out the rhythm section of *Ol' Man River*.

Nothing.

And nothing I could do till morning.

The next day I leapt out of bed determined to explain to my mother what was wrong.

There was no one in the house.

My breakfast had been left on the kitchenette with a short note.

'Dear Jeanette,

We have gone to the hospital to pray for Auntie Betty. Her leg is very loose.

Love mother.'

So I spent the day as well as I could, and finally decided to go for a walk. That walk was my salvation. I met Miss Jewsbury who played the oboe and conducted the Sisterhood choir. She was very clever.

'But she's not holy,' Mrs White had once said. Miss Jewsbury must have said hello to me, and I must have ignored her. She hadn't been to church for a long time because of her tour of the Midlands with the Salvation Symphony Orchestra, and so she didn't know that I was supposed to be full of the spirit. She stood in front of me opening and shutting her mouth, which was very large on account of the oboe, and pulling her eyebrows into the middle of her head. I took hold of her hand and led her into the post office. Then I picked up one of the pens and wrote on the back of a child allowance form,

'Dear Miss Jewsbury,

I can't hear a thing.'

She looked at me in horror and, taking the pen herself, wrote, 'What is your mother doing about it? Why aren't you in bed?'

By now there was no room left on the child allowance form so I had to use Who to Contact in the Event of An Emergency.

'Dear Miss Jewsbury,' I wrote,

'My mother doesn't know. She's at the hospital with Auntie Betty. I was in bed last night.'

Miss Jewsbury just stared and stared. She stared for so long I began to think about going home. Then she snatched my hand and whisked me off to the hospital. When we got there my mother and some others were gathered around Auntie Betty's bed singing choruses. My mother saw us, looked a bit surprised, but didn't get up. Miss Jewsbury tapped her on the elbow, and started doing the routine with her mouth and eyebrows. My mother just shook and shook her head. Finally Miss Jewsbury yelled so loud even I heard it. 'This child's not full of the Spirit,' she screamed, 'she's deaf.'

Everyone in the hospital turned to peer at me. I went very red, and stared at Auntie Betty's water jug. The worst thing was not knowing at all what was going on. Then a doctor came over to us, very angry, and then he and Miss Jewsbury waved their arms at each other. The Faithful had gone back to their chorus sheets as though nothing was happening at all.

The doctor and Miss Jewsbury whisked me away to a cold room full of equipment, and made me lie down. The doctor kept tapping me in different places and shaking his head.

And it was all absolutely silent.

Then my mother arrived and seemed to understand what was going on. She signed a form, and wrote me another note.

'Dear Jeanette,

There's nothing wrong, you're just a bit deaf. Why didn't you tell me? I'm going home to get your pyjamas.'

What was she doing? Why was she leaving me here? I started to cry. My mother looked horrified and rooting in her handbag she gave me an orange. I peeled it to comfort myself, and seeing me a little calmer, everyone glanced at one another and went away.

Since I was born I had assumed that the world ran on very simple lines, like a larger version of our church. Now I was finding that even the church was sometimes confused. This was a problem. But not one I chose to deal with for many years more. The problem there and then was what was going to happen to me. The Victoria Hospital was big and frightening, and I couldn't even sing to any effect because I couldn't hear what I was singing. There was nothing to read except some dental notices and an instruction leaflet for the X-ray machine. I tried to build an igloo out of the orange peel but it kept falling down and even when it stood up I didn't have an eskimo to put in it, so I had to invent a story about 'How Eskimo Got Eaten', which made me even more miserable. It's always the same with diversions; you get involved.

At last my mother came back, and a nurse pulled me into my pyjamas and took us both to the children's ward. It was horrid. The walls were pale pink and all the curtains had animals on them. Not real animals though: fluffy ones playing games with coloured balls.

I thought of the sea walrus I had just invented. It was wicked, it had eaten the eskimo; but it was better than these. The nurse had thrown my igloo in the bin.

There was nothing for me to do but contemplate my fate and lie still. A couple of hours later my mother returned with my Bible, a Scripture Union colouring book, and a wedge of plasticine, which the nurse took away. I pulled a face, and she wrote on a card, 'Not nice, might swallow.' I looked at her and wrote back, 'I don't want to swallow it, I want to build with it. Besides plasticine isn't toxic, it tells you on the back,' and I waved the packet at her. She frowned and shook her head. I turned to my mother for support, but she was scribbling me a long letter. The nurse started to rearrange my bed, and put the offending putty in her uniform pocket. I could see that nothing would change her mind.

I sniffed; disinfectant and mashed potatoes. Then my mother prodded me, put her letter on the bedside cabinet, and emptied a huge carrier bag of oranges into the bowl by my water jug. I smiled feebly, hoping to gain support, but instead she patted me on the head and rolled away. So I was alone. I thought of Jane Eyre, who faced many trials and was always brave. My mother read the book to me whenever she felt sad; she said it gave her fortitude. I picked up her letter: the usual not-to-worry, lots-of-people-will-visit, chin-up, and a promise to work hard on the bathroom, and not let Mrs White get in the way. That she'd come soon, or if not she'd send her husband. That my operation would be the next day. At this, I let the letter fall to the bed. The next day! What if I died? So young and so promising! I thought of my funeral, of all the tears. I wanted to be buried with Golly and my Bible. Should I write instructions? Could I count on any of them to take any notice? My mother knew all about illness and operations. The doctor had told her that a woman in her condition shouldn't be walking around, but she said that her time hadn't come, and at least she knew where she was going, not like him. My mother read in a book that more people die under anaesthetic than drown while water-skiing.

'If the Lord brings you back,' she told May, before she went in for her gallstones, 'you'll know it's because he's got work for you to do.' I crept under the bedclothes and prayed to be brought back.

On the morning of my operation, the nurses were smiling and rearranging the bed again, and piling the oranges in a symmetrical tower. Two hairy arms lifted me up and strapped me on to a cold trolley. The castors squeaked and the man who pushed me went too fast. Corridors, double doors and two pairs of eyes peeping over the top of tight white masks. A nurse held my hand while someone fitted a muzzle over my nose and mouth. I breathed in and saw a great line of water-skiers falling off and not coming back up. Then I didn't see anything at all.

'Jelly, Jeanette.'

I *knew* it, I'd died and the angels were giving me jelly. I opened my eyes expecting to see a pair of wings.

'Come on, eat up,' the voice encouraged.

'Are you an angel?' I asked hopefully.

'Not quite, I'm a doctor. But she's an angel, aren't you nurse?'

The angel blushed.

'I can hear,' I said, to no one in particular.

'Eat your jelly,' said the nurse.

I might have languished alone for the rest of the week, if Elsie hadn't found out where I was, and started visiting me. My mother couldn't come till the weekend, I knew that, because she was waiting for the plumber to check her fittings. Elsie came every day, and told me jokes to make me smile and stories to make me feel better. She said stories helped you to understand the world. When I felt better, she promised to show me the basics I needed to help her with numerology. A thrill of excitement ran through me because I knew my mother disapproved. She said it was too close to madness.

'Never mind that,' said Elsie, 'it works.'

So we had quite a good time, the two of us, planning what we'd do when I got better.

'How old are you Elsie?' I wanted to know.

'I remember the Great War, and that's all I'm saying.' Then she started to tell me how she'd driven an ambulance without any brakes.

My mother came to see me quite a lot in the end, but it was the busy season at church. They were planning the Christmas campaign. When she couldn't come herself she sent my father, usually with a letter and a couple of oranges.

'The only fruit,' she always said.

Fruit salad, fruit pie, fruit for fools, fruited punch. Demon fruit, passion fruit, rotten fruit, fruit on Sunday.

Oranges are the only fruit. I filled my little bucket with peel and the nurses emptied it with an ill grace. I hid the peel under my pillow and the nurses scolded and sighed.

Elsie Norris and me ate an orange every day; half

each. Elsie had no teeth so she sucked and champed. I dropped my pieces like oysters, far back into the throat. People used to watch us, but we didn't mind.

When Elsie wasn't reading the Bible, or telling stories, she spent time with the poets. She told me all about Swinburne and his troubles, and about the oppression of William Blake.

'No one listens to eccentrics,' she said. When I was sad she read me *Goblin Market* by a woman called Christina Rossetti, whose friend once gave her a pickled mouse in a jar, for a present.

But of all her loves, Elsie's favourite was W. B. Yeats. Yeats, she said, knew the importance of numbers, and the great effect of the imagination on the world.

'What looks like one thing,' she told me, 'may well be another.' I was reminded of my orange peel igloo.

'If you think about something for long enough,' she explained, 'more than likely, that thing will happen.' She tapped her head. 'It's all in the mind.'

My mother believed that if you prayed for something long enough it happened. I asked Elsie if that was the same thing.

'God's in everything,' she said thoughtfully, 'so it's always the same thing.'

I had a feeling my mother would disagree, but she wasn't there, so it didn't matter.

I played Ludo with Elsie, and Hang the Man, and she took to reading me a poem just before she left at the end of visiting time.

One of them had these lines in it:

'All things fall and are built again
And those that build them again are gay.'

I understood this because I had been working on my orange peel igloo for weeks. Some days were a great disappointment, others, a near triumph. It was a feat of balance and vision. Elsie was always encouraging, and told me not to mind the nurses.

'It would have been easier with plasticine,' I complained one day.

'But less interesting,' she said.

When I finally left the hospital, my hearing had been restored, and my confidence recovered (thanks to her).

I had to go and stay with Elsie for a couple of days, until my mother got home from Wigan, where she was auditing the Society for the Lost.

'I've found a new piece of sheet music,' she said on the bus, 'it's got an interlude for seven elephants in it.'

'What's it called?'

The Battle of Abysinnia.

Which is, of course, a very famous bit of Victorian Sentiment, like Prince Albert.

'Anything else?'

'Not really, the Lord and I don't bother with each other just now. It comes and goes, so I've been doing a bit of decorating while I can. Nothing fancy, just a dab on the skirting boards, but when I'm with the Lord, I haven't time for anything!'

When we got home, she came over all mysterious, and told me to wait in the parlour. I could hear her rustling and muttering, then I heard something squeaking. At last she pushed open the door, wheezing loudly.

'God forgive me,' she panted, 'but it's a bugger.'

And she plonked a large box on the table.

'Open it then.'

'What is it?'

'Never mind that, open it.'

I pulled off the wrapper.

It was a domed wooden box with three white mice inside.

'Shadrach, Meshach and Abednego in the fiery furnace.' She stretched her gums at me into a smile. 'Look, I painted them flames meself.'

The back of the box was a wash of angry orange paint shaped into tongues of flame.

'It could even be Pentecost,' I suggested.

'Oh yes, it's very versatile,' she agreed.

The mice took no notice.

'And see, I made these too.' She shuffled in her bag and pulled out two plywood figures. They were both painted very bright, but it was obvious that one was celestial, from the wings. She looked at me, triumphant.

'Nebuchadnezzar and the angel of the Lord.'

The angel had little slits in his base that helped him to fit on top of the dome without disturbing the mice.

'It's beautiful,' I said.

'I know,' she nodded, dropping a bit of cheese past the angel.

That evening we made some scones and sat by the fire. She had an old fireplace with pictures of famous men and Florence Nightingale printed on to the tiles. Clive of India was there, and Palmerston, and Sir Isaac Newton with a singed chin where the fire roared too high. Elsie showed me her holy dice, bought in Mecca forty years ago. She kept them in a box behind the chimney breast, in case of thieves.

'Some folks say I'm a fool, but there's more to this world than meets the eye.' I waited quietly.

'There's this world,' she banged the wall graphically, 'and there's this world,' she thumped her chest. 'If you want to make sense of either, you have to take notice of both.'

'I don't understand,' I sighed, thinking what to ask next, to make it clearer, but she had fallen asleep with her mouth open, and besides, there were the mice to feed.

Perhaps I'll find out when I get to school was my only consolation as the hours ticked past and Elsie didn't wake up. Even when she did wake up, she seemed to have forgotten all about her explanation of the universe, and wanted to build a tunnel for the mice. I didn't find many explanations at school though either; it only got more and more complex. After three terms I was beginning to despair. I'd learnt country dancing and the rudiments of needlework, but not a great deal more. Country dancing was thirty-three rickety kids in black plimsolls and green knickers trying to keep up with Miss who always danced with Sir anyway and never looked at anybody else. They got engaged soon after, but it didn't do us any good because they started going in for ballroom competitions, which meant they spent all our lessons practising their footwork while we shuffled up and down to the recorded instructions on the gramophone. The threats were the worst; being forced to hold hands with somebody you hated. We flapped along twisting each others' fingers off and promising untold horrors as soon as the lesson was over. Tired of being bullied, I became adept at inventing the most fundamental tortures under the guise of sweet sainthood. 'What me Miss? No Miss. Oh *Miss*, I never did.' But I did, I always did.

The most frightening for the girls was the offer of total immersion in the cesspit round the back of Rathbone's Wrought Iron. For the boys, anything that involved their willies. And so, three terms later, I squatted down in the shoebags and got depressed. The shoebag room was dark and smelly, it was always smelly, even at the beginning of terms.

'You can't get rid of feet,' I heard the caretaker say sourly.

The cleaning lady shook her head; she'd got rid of more smells than she's eaten hot dinners. She had even worked in a zoo once, 'and you know how them animals stink,' but the feet had beaten her. 'This stuff takes the seal off floors,' she said, waving a red tin, 'but it don't shift feet.'

We didn't really notice after a week or so, and besides it was a good place to hide. The teachers didn't come near it, except to supervise a few yards away from the door. The last day of term . . . we'd been on a school trip to Chester Zoo earlier in the week. That meant everybody in their Sunday best, vying for who had the cleanest socks and the most impressive sand-wiches. Canned drinks were our envy, since most of us had orange squash in Tupperware pots. The Tupperware always heated up, and burnt our mouths.

'You've got brown bread' (scuffling over the seats come three heads). 'What that for? It's got bits in it, you vegetarian?'

I try not to take any notice as my sandwiches are prodded. The general sandwich inspection continues from seat to seat, alternating between murmurs of envy and shrieks of laughter. Susan Green had cold fish fingers in hers, because her family were very poor and had to eat leftovers even if they were horrible. Last time she'd only had brown sauce, because there weren't even any leftovers. The inspectorate decided that Shelley had the best. Bright white rolls stuffed with curried egg and a dash of parsley. And she had a can of lemonade. The zoo itself was not exciting and we had to walk in twos. Our crocodile weaved in and out, ruining new shoes with sand and sawdust, sweating and sticking to each other. Stanley Farmer slipped into the flamingo pond, and nobody had any money to buy model animals. So an hour early, we trooped back on to our coach, and joggled home. Three plastic bags full of sick and hundreds of sweet wrappers were our memento to the driver. It was all we could part with.

'Never again,' heaved Mrs Virtue, herding us out on to the street. 'Never again will I risk disgrace.'

Right now Mrs Virtue was helping Shelley finish her summer party dress. 'They deserve each other,' I thought.

I comforted myself with the thought of the summer camp our church went on each year. This time we were going far away, to Devon. My mother was very excited because Pastor Spratt had promised to call in on one of his rare visits to England. He was to take the first Sunday service in the gospel tent just outside Cullompton. At the moment Pastor Spratt was touring his exhibition in Europe. He was fast becoming one of the most famous and successful missionaries that our group of churches had ever sent out. Tribesmen from places we couldn't pronounce sent thank-you letters to our headquarters, rejoicing in the Lord and their new salvation. To celebrate his ten thousandth convert, the pastor had been funded to take a long holiday and tour his collection of weapons, amulets, idols and primitive methods of contraception. The exhibition was called 'Saved by Grace Alone'. I had only seen the leaflet, but my mother had all the details. Apart from Pastor Spratt, we had planned a careful campaign for the farming folk of Devon. In the past we had always used the same techniques, whether in a tent or in a town hall, and regardless of the location. Then, our campaigns secretary had received an action kit from Headquarters, explaining that the Second Coming might be at any time, and it was up to us to put all our efforts into saving souls. The action kit, which had been specially designed by the Charismatic Movement Marketing Council, explained that people are different and need a different approach. You had to make salvation relevant to them, to their minds. So, if you visited a sea people, you used sea metaphors to pass on the message. And most important, when talking to individuals, you determined as soon as you could what they most wanted in life, and of what they were most afraid. This made the message immediately relevant. The Council set us training weekends for all those engaged in the Good Fight, and gave out graphs so that we could monitor any improvements, and be encouraged. Pastor Spratt had written a personal recommendation on the back of the kits. There was a photo of him too, much younger, baptising a chief. So, our aim was to prove the Lord relevant to the farming folk of Devon. My mother was in charge of the camp stores, and had already started to buy in huge tins of beans and frankfurter sausages. 'An army marches on its stomach,' she told me.

We were hoping to make enough converts to start a new church in Exeter.

'I remember when we built the gospel hall here,' said my mother wistfully. 'All of us pulling together, and we only used born-again workmen.' It had been a bright, difficult time; saving up for a piano and hymn books; fending off the temptations of the Devil to go on holiday instead.

'Of course, your father was a card player in those days.'

Eventually they had got a grant from head office to finish the roof, and pay for a flag to fly from the top. It was a proud day when they hoisted the flag, with SEEK YE THE LORD embroidered in red letters. All the churches had flags, made by disabled missionaries. It was a way of helping out their pension and giving them spiritual satisfaction. During the first year my mother had gone into all the pubs and clubs urging the drunkards to join her at church. She used to sit at the piano and sing *Have You Any Room for Jesus?* It was very moving, she said. The men cried into their tankards and stopped playing snooker while she sang. She was plump and pretty and they called her the Jesus Belle.

'Oh, I had my offers,' she confided, 'and they weren't all Godly.' Whatever they were, the church grew, and many a man will stop in the street when my mother goes past and raise his hat to the Jesus Belle.

Sometimes I think she married in haste. After her awful time with Pierre she wanted no more upsets. When I sat by her looking through the photograph album at ancestors with stern faces, she always stopped at the two pages called 'Old Flames' in the index.

Pierre was there, and others including my father. 'Why didn't you marry that one, or that one?' I asked, curious.

'They were all wayward men,' she sighed. 'I had a bad time enough finding one that was only a gambler.'

'Why isn't he a gambler now?' I wanted to know, trying to imagine my meek father looking like the men I'd seen on films.

'He married me and he found the Lord.' Then she sighed and told me the story of each one of the Old Flames; Mad Percy, who drove an open-topped car and asked her to live with him in Brighton; Eddy with the tortoiseshell glasses who kept bees . . . right at the bottom of the page was a yellowy picture of a pretty woman holding a cat.

'Who's that?' I pointed.

'That? Oh just Eddy's sister, I don't know why I put it there,' and she turned the page. Next time we looked, it had gone.

So she married my father and reformed him and he built the church and never got angry. I thought he was nice, though he didn't say much. Of course, her own father was furious. He told her she'd married down, that she should have stayed in Paris, and promptly ended all communication. So she never had enough money and after a while she managed to forget that she'd ever had any at all. 'The church is my family,' she always said whenever I asked about the people in the photograph album. And the church was my family too.

At school I couldn't seem to learn anything or win anything, not even the draw to get out of being dinner monitor. Dinner monitor meant that you had to make sure everybody had a plate and that the water jug didn't have bits in it. Dinner monitors got served last and had the smallest portions. I'd been drawn to do it three times running and I got shouted at in class for always smelling of gravy. My clothes were gravy-spotted and my mother made me wear the same gymslip all week because she said there was no point trying to make me look clean as long as I had that duty. Now I was sitting in the shoebags, with liver and onions all down my front. Sometimes I tried to clean it off, but today I was too unhappy. After six weeks' holiday with our church, I'd be even less able to cope with any of it. My mother was right. It was a Breeding Ground. And it wasn't as though I hadn't tried. At first I'd done my very best to fit in and be good. We had been set a project just before we started last autumn, we had to write an essay called 'What I Did in my Summer Holidays'. I was anxious to do it well because I knew they thought I couldn't read or anything, not having been to school early enough. I did it slowly in my best handwriting, proud that some of the others could only print. We read them out one by one, then gave them to the teacher. It was all the same, fishing, swimming, picnics, Walt Disney. Thirty-two essays about gardens and frog spawn. I was at the end of the alphabet, and I could hardly wait. The teacher was the kind of woman who wanted her class to be happy. She called us lambs, and told me in particular not to worry if I found anything difficult.

'You'll soon fit in,' she soothed.

I wanted to please her, and trembling with antici-pation I started my essay . . . '"This holiday I went to Colwyn Bay with our church camp."'

The teacher nodded and smiled.

"'It was very hot, and Auntie Betty, whose leg was loose anyway, got sunstroke and we thought she might die.'"

The teacher began to look a bit worried, but the class perked up.

"'But she got better, thanks to my mother who stayed up all night struggling mightily.'"

'Is your mother a nurse?' asked the teacher, with quiet sympathy.

'No, she just heals the sick.'

Teacher frowned. 'Well, carry on then.'

"'When Auntie Betty got better we all went in the bus to Llandudno to testify on the beach. I played the tambourine, and Elsie Norris brought her accordian, but a boy threw some sand, and since then she's had no F sharp. We're going to have a jumble sale in the autumn to try and pay for it.

"'When we came back from Colwyn Bay, Next Door had had another baby but there are so many of them Next Door we don't know whose it is. My mother gave them some potatoes from the yard, but they said they weren't a charity and threw them back over the wall.'"

The class had gone very quiet. Teacher looked at me.

'Is there any more?'

'Yes, two more sides.'

'What about?'

'Not much, just how we hired the baths for our baptism service after the Healing of the Sick crusade.'

'Very good, but I don't think we'll have time today. Put your work back in your tidy box, and do some colouring till playtime.'

The class giggled.

Slowly I sat down, not sure what was going on, but sure that something was. When I got home I told my mother I didn't want to go again.

'You've got to,' she said. 'Here, have an orange.'

Some weeks passed, in which I tried to make myself as ordinary as possible. It seemed like it was working, and then we started sewing class; on Wednesdays, after toad-in-the-hole and Manchester tart. We did our cross stitch and chain stitch and then we had to think of a project. I decided to make a sampler for Elsie Norris. The girl next to me wanted to do one for her mother, TO MOTHER WITH LOVE; the girl opposite a birthday motif. When it came to me I said I wanted a text.

'What about SUFFER LITTLE CHILDREN?' suggested Mrs Virtue.

I knew that wouldn't do for Elsie. She liked the prophets.

'No,' I said firmly, 'it's for my friend, and she reads Jeremiah mostly. I was thinking of THE SUMMER IS ENDED AND WE ARE NOT YET SAVED.'

Mrs Virtue was a diplomatic woman, but she had her blind spots. When it came to listing all the samplers, she wrote the others out in full, and next to mine put 'Text'.

'Why's that?' I asked.

'You might upset the others,' she said. 'Now what colour do you want, yellow, green, or red?'

We looked at each other.

'Black,' I said.

I did upset the children. Not intentionally, but effectively. Mrs Sparrow and Mrs Spencer came to

school one day all fluffed up with rage; they came
at playtime, I saw them with their handbags and hats,
revolving up the concrete, lips pursed. Mrs Spencer
had her gloves on.

Some of the others knew what was happening.
There was a little group of them by the fence, whis-
pering. One of them pointed at me. I tried not to
notice and carried on with my whip and top. The
group got bigger, a girl with sherbet on her mouth
yelled across at me, I didn't catch what she said, but
the others all screamed with laughter. Then a boy
came and hit me on the neck, then another and
another, all hitting and running off.

'Tag, tag,' they cried as the teacher came past.

I was bewildered, then angry, in-the-stomach angry.
I caught one with my little whip. He yelped.

'Miss, Miss, she hit me.'

'Miss, Miss, she hit him,' chorused the rest.

Miss took me by the back of my hair and hauled
me off inside.

Outside, the bell rang, there was noise and doors
and scuffling, then quiet. That particular corridor quiet.

I was in the staff room.

Miss turned to me, she looked tired.

'Hold out your hand.'

I held out my hand.

She reached for the ruler. I thought of the Lord.
The staff room door opened, and in walked Mrs Vole,
the head.

'Ah, I see Jeanette is here already. Wait outside a
moment, will you?'

I withdrew my sacrificial palm, shoved it into my
pocket and slid out between them.

I was just in time to see the retreating shapes of Mrs Spencer and Mrs Sparrow, ripe plums of indignation falling from them.

It was cold in the corridor; I could hear low voices behind the door, but nothing happened. I started to pick at the radiator with my compass, trying to make a bit of warped plastic look like Paris from the air.

Last night at church had been the prayer meeting, and Mrs White had had a vision.

'What was it like?' we asked eagerly.

'Oh, it was very holy,' said Mrs White.

The plans for the Christmas campaign were well under way. We had got permission from the Salvation Army to share their crib space outside the town hall, and rumour had it that Pastor Spratt might be back with some of the converted Heathen. 'We can only hope and pray,' said my mother, writing to him at once.

I had won yet another Bible quiz competition, and to my great relief had been picked as narrator for the Sunday School Pageant. I had been Mary for the last three years, and there was nothing else I could bring to the part. Besides, it meant playing opposite Stanley Farmer.

It was clear and warm and made me happy.

At school there was only confusion.

By this time I had squatted on the floor, so when the door finally opened all I could see were wool stockings and Hush Puppies.

'We'd like to talk to you,' said Mrs Vole.

I scrambled up and went inside, feeling like Daniel.

Mrs Vole picked up an ink well, and looked at me carefully.

'Jeanette, we think you may be having problems at school. Do you want to tell us about them?'

'I'm all right.' I shuffled defensively.

'You do seem rather pre-occupied, shall we say, with God.'

I continued to stare at the floor.

'Your sampler, for instance, had a very disturbing motif.'

'It was for my friend, she liked it,' I burst out, thinking how Elsie's face had lit up when I had given it to her.

'And who is your friend?'

'She's called Elsie Norris and she gave me three mice in the fiery furnace.'

Mrs Vole and Miss looked at one another.

'And why did you choose to write about hoopoos and rock badgers in your animal book, and in one case, I believe, shrimps?'

'My mother taught me to read,' I told them rather desperately.

'Yes, your reading skills are quite unusual, but you haven't answered my question.'

How could I?

My mother had taught me to read from the Book of Deuteronomy because it is full of animals (mostly unclean). Whenever we read 'Thou shall not eat any beast that does not chew the cud or part the hoof' she drew all the creatures mentioned. Horsies, bunnies and little ducks were vague fabulous things, but I knew all about pelicans, rock badgers, sloths and bats. This tendency towards the exotic has brought me many problems, just as it did for William Blake. My mother drew winged insects, and the birds of the air, but my favourite ones were the seabed ones, the molluscs. I had a fine collection from the beach at Blackpool. She had a blue pen for the waves, and brown ink for the scaly-backed crab. Lobsters were red biro, she never drew shrimps, though, because she liked to eat them in a muffin. I think it had troubled her for a long time. Finally, after much prayer, and some consultation with a great man of the Lord in Shrewsbury, she agreed with St Paul that what God has cleansed we must not call common. After that we went to Molly's seafoods every Saturday. Deuteronomy had its drawbacks; it's full of Abominations and Unmentionables. Whenever we read about a bastard, or someone with crushed testicles, my mother turned over the page and said, 'Leave that to the Lord,' but when she'd gone, I'd sneak a look. I was glad I didn't have testicles. They sounded like intestines only on the outside, and the men in the Bible were always having them cut off and not being able to go to church. Horrid.

'Well,' pressed Mrs Vole, 'I'm waiting.'

'I don't know,' I replied.

'And why, and this is perhaps more serious, do you terrorize, yes, terrorize, the other children?'

'I don't,' I protested.

'Then can you tell me why I had Mrs Spencer and Mrs Sparrow here this morning telling me how their children have nightmares?'

'I have nightmares too.'

'That's not the point. You have been talking about Hell to young minds.'

It was true. I couldn't deny it. I had told all the others about the horrors of the demon and the fate

of the damned. I had illustrated it by almost strangling Susan Hunt, but that was an accident, and I gave
her all my cough sweets afterwards.

'I'm very sorry,' I said, 'I thought it was interesting.'

Mrs Vole and Miss shook their heads.

'You'd better go,' said Mrs Vole. 'I shall be writing
to your mother.'

I was very depressed. What was all the fuss about?
Better to hear about Hell now than burn in it later.
I walked past Class 3's collage of an Easter bunny, and
I thought of Elsie's collage of Noah's Ark, with the
removable chimp.

It was obvious where I belonged. Ten more years
and I could go to missionary school.

Mrs Vole kept her promise. She wrote to my mother,
explaining my religious leanings, and asking my
mother if she would moderate me. My mother hooted
and took me to the cinema as a treat. They were
showing *The Ten Commandments*. I asked if Elsie could
come, but my mother said no.

After that day, everyone at school avoided me. If it
had not been for the conviction that I was right, I
might have been very sad. As it was I just forgot about
it, did my lessons as best I could, which wasn't that
well, and thought about our church. I told my mother
how things were once.

'We are called to be apart,' she said.

My mother didn't have many friends either. People
didn't understand the way she thought; neither did I,
but I loved her because she always knew exactly why
things happened.

★

When it came round to Prizegiving, I took my sampler back from Elsie Norris and entered it for the needle-work class. I still think it was a masterpiece of its kind; it had the lettering all in black, and the border all in white, and in the bottom corner a sort of artist's impression of the terrified damned. Elsie had framed it, so it looked quite professional.

Mrs Virtue stood at the top of the class, collecting . . .

'Irene, yes.'

'Vera, yes.'

'Shelley, yes.' (Shelley was a Brownie.)

'Here's mine Mrs Virtue,' I said, placing it on the desk.

'Yes,' she said, meaning No.

'I will enter it, if that's what you want, but to be frank I don't think it's the sort of thing the judges will be hoping for.'

'What do you mean,' I demanded, 'it's got every-thing, adventure, pathos, mystery . . .'

She interrupted.

'I mean, your use of colour is limited, you don't exploit the potential of the thread; take Shelley's Village Scene, for instance, notice the variety, the colours.'

'She's used four colours, I've used three.'

Mrs Virtue frowned.

'And besides, no one else has used black.'

Mrs Virtue sat down.

'And I've used mythical counter-relief,' I insisted, pointing at the terrified damned.

Mrs Virtue laid her head on her hands.

'What are you talking about? If you mean that messy blotch in the corner . . .'

I was furious; luckily I had been reading about how Sir Joshua Reynolds insulted Turner.

'Just because you can't tell what it is, doesn't mean it's not what it is.'

I picked up Shelley's Village Scene.

'That doesn't look like a sheep, it's all white and fluffy.'

'Go back to your desk, Jeanette.'

'But . . .'

'GO BACK TO YOUR DESK!'

What could I do? My needlework teacher suffered from a problem of vision. She recognized things according to expectation and environment. If you were in a particular place, you expected to see particular things. Sheep and hills, sea and fish; if there was an elephant in the supermarket, she'd either not see it at all, or call it Mrs Jones and talk about fish-cakes. But most likely, she'd do what most people do when confronted with something they don't understand:

Panic.

What constitutes a problem is not the thing, or the environment where we find the thing, but the conjunction of the two; something unexpected in an usual place (our favourite aunt in our favourite poker parlour) or something usual in an unexpected place (our favourite poker in our favourite aunt). I knew that my sampler was absolutely right in Elsie Norris's front room, but absolutely wrong in Mrs Virtue's sewing class. Mrs Virtue should either have had the imagination to commend me for my effort in context, or the farsightedness to realize that there is a debate going on as to whether something has an absolute as well as a relative value; given that, she should have given me the benefit of the doubt.

As it was she got upset and blamed me for her headache. This was very like Sir Joshua Reynolds, who complained that Turner always gave him a headache.

I didn't win anything with my sampler though, and I was very disappointed. I took it back to Elsie on the last day of school and asked her if she still wanted it.

She snatched it from me, and put it firmly on the wall.

'It's upside down, Elsie,' I pointed out.

She fumbled for her glasses, and stared at it.

'So it is, but it's all the same to the Lord. Still, I'll put it right for them that doesn't know.'

And she carefully adjusted the picture.

'I thought you might not like it any more.'

'Heathen child, the Lord himself was scorned, don't expect the unwashed to appreciate.'

(Elsie always called the unconverted the unwashed.)

'Well it would be nice sometimes,' I ventured, displaying a tendency towards relativism.

Elsie got very cross. She was an absolutist, and had no time for people who thought cows didn't exist unless you looked at them. Once a thing was created, it was valid for all time. Its value went not up nor down.

Perception, she said was a fraud; had not St Paul said we see in a glass darkly, had not Wordsworth said we see by glimpses? 'This piece of fruit cake' – she waved it between bites – 'this cake doesn't need me to eat it to make it edible. It exists without me.'

That was a bad example, but I knew what she meant. It meant that to create was a fundament, to appreciate, a supplement. Once created, the creature was separate from the creator, and needed no seconding to fully exist.

'Have some cake,' she said cheerfully, but I didn't because even if Elsie was philosophically amiss, her contention that the cake existed without either of us was certainly true. There was probably a whole township in there, with values of its own, and a style of gossip.

Over the years I did my best to win a prize; some wish to better the world and still scorn it. But I never succeeded; there's a formula, a secret, I don't know what, that people who have been to public school or Brownies seem to understand. It runs right the way through life, though it starts with hyacinth growing, passes through milk monitor, and finishes somewhere at half-blue.

My hyacinths were pink. Two of them. I called the ensemble 'The Annunciation' (you have to have a theme). This was because the blooms were huddled up close, and reminded me of Mary and Elizabeth soon after the visit by the angel. I thought it was a very clever marriage of horticulture and theology. I put a little explanation at the bottom, and the appropriate verse so that people could look it up if they wanted to, but it didn't win. What did win was a straggly white pair called 'Snow Sisters'. So I took 'The Annunciation' home and fed it to our rabbit. I was a bit uneasy afterwards in case it was heresy, and the rabbit fell sick. Later, I tried to win the Easter egg painting competition. I had had so little success with my biblical themes that it seemed an idea to try something new. It couldn't be anything pre-Raphaelite, because Janey Morris was thin, and not suited to being played by an egg.

Coleridge and the Man from Porlock?

Coleridge was fat, but I felt the tableau would lack dramatic interest.

'It's obvious,' said Elsie. 'Wagner.'

So we cut a cardboard box to set the scene, Elsie doing the back-drop, me doing the rocks out of half-egg shells. We stayed up all night on the dramatis personae, because of the detail. We had chosen the most exciting bit, 'Brunhilda Confronts Her Father'. I did Brunhilda, and Elsie did Wodin. Brunhilda had a helmet made out of a thimble with little feather wings from Elsie's pillow.

'She needs a spear,' said Elsie, 'I'll give you a cock-tail stick only don't tell anyone what I use it for.'

As a final touch I cut off some of my own hair and made it into Brunhilda's hair.

Wodin was a masterpiece, a double-yolker brown egg, with a Ritz cracker shield and a drawn-on eye-patch. We made him a match-box chariot that was just too small.

'Dramatic emphasis,' said Elsie.

The next day I took it to school and placed it beside the others; there was no comparison. Imagine my horror when it didn't win. I was not a selfish child and, understanding the nature of genius, would have happily bowed to another's talent, but not to three eggs covered in cotton wool, entitled 'Easter Bunnies'.

'It's not fair,' I told Elsie, later that same evening at the Sisterhood meeting.

'You'll get used to it.'

'And anyway,' butted in Mrs White, who had heard the story, 'they're not holy.'

I didn't despair; I did *Streetcar Named Desire* out of pipe-cleaners, an embroidered cushion cover of Bette Davis in *Now Voyager*, an oregami William Tell with real apple, and best of all, a potato sculpture of Henry Ford outside the Chrysler building in New York. An impressive list by any standards, but I was as hopeful and as foolish as King Canute forcing back the waves. Whatever I did made no impression at all, except to enrage my mother because I had abandoned biblical themes. She quite liked *Now Voyager*, because she had done her courting during that film, but she thought I should have made the Tower of Babel out of oregami, even though I told her it would be too difficult.

'The Lord walked on the water,' was all she said when I tried to explain. But she had her own problems. A lot of the missionaries had been eaten, which meant she had to explain to their families.

'It's not easy,' she said, 'even though it's for the Lord.'

When the children of Israel left Egypt, they were guided by the pillar of cloud by day, and the pillar of fire by night. For them, this did not seem to be a problem. For me, it was an enormous problem. The pillar of cloud was a fog, perplexing and impossible. I didn't understand the ground rules. The daily world was a world of Strange Notions, without form, and therefore void. I comforted myself as best I could by always rearranging their version of the facts.

One day, I learned that Tetrahedron is a mathematical

shape that can be formed by stretching an elastic band over a series of nails.

But Tetrahedron is an emperor . . .

The emperor Tetrahedron lived in a palace made absolutely from elastic bands. To the right, cunning fountains shot elastic jets, subtle as silk; to the left, ten minstrels played day and night on elastic lutes.

The emperor was beloved by all.

At night, when the thin dogs slept, and the music lulled all but the most watchful to sleep, the mighty palace lay closed and barred against the foul Isosceles, sworn enemy to the graceful Tetrahedron.

But in the day, the guards pulled back the great doors, flooding the plain with light, so that gifts could be brought to the emperor.

Many brought gifts; stretches of material so fine that a change of the temperature would dissolve it; stretches of material so strong that whole cities could be built from it.

And stories of love and folly.

One day, a lovely woman brought the emperor a revolving circus operated by midgets.

The midgets acted all of the tragedies and many of the comedies. They acted them all at once, and it was fortunate that Tetrahedron had so many faces, otherwise he might have died of fatigue.

They acted them all at once, and the emperor, walking round his theatre, could see them all at once, if he wished.

Round and round he walked, and so learned a very valuable thing:

that no emotion is the final one.

LEVITICUS

THE HEATHEN WERE a daily household preoccupation. My mother found them everywhere, particularly Next Door. They tormented her as only the godless can, but she had her methods.

They hated hymns, and she liked to play the piano, an old upright with pitted candelabra and yellow keys. We each had a copy of the *Redemption Hymnal* (boards and cloth 3 shillings). My mother sang the tune, and I put in the harmonies. The first hymn I ever learned was a magnificent Victorian composition called *Ask the Saviour to Help You*.

One Sunday morning, just as we got in from Communion, we heard strange noises, like cries for help, coming from Next Door. I took no notice, but my mother froze behind the radiogram, and started to change colour. Mrs White, who had come home with us to listen to the World Service, immediately crushed her ear against the wall.

'What is it?' I asked.

'I don't know,' she said in loud whisper, 'but whatever it is, it's not holy.'

Still my mother didn't move.

'Have you got a wine glass?' urged Mrs White.

My mother looked horrified.

'For medicinal purposes, I mean,' added Mrs White hurriedly.

My mother went into a high cupboard, and reached down a box from the top shelf. This was her War Cupboard, and every week she bought a new tin to put in it, in case of the Holocaust. Mostly it was full of black cherries in syrup and special offer sardines.

'I never use these,' she said meaningfully.

'Neither do I,' said Mrs White defensively, clamping herself back against the wall. While my mother was covering up the television, Mrs White slithered up and down the skirting board.

'We've just had that wall decorated,' my mother pointed out.

'It's stopped anyway,' panted Mrs White.

At that moment another burst of wailing began from Next Door.

Very clear this time.

'They're fornicating,' cried my mother, rushing to put her hands over my ears.

'Get off,' I yelled.

The dog started barking, and my dad, who had been on nights the Saturday just gone, came down in his pyjama bottoms.

'Put some clothes on,' shrieked my mother, 'Next Door's at it again.'

I bit my mother's hand. 'Let go of my ears, I can hear it too.'

'On a Sunday,' exclaimed Mrs White.

Outside, suddenly, the ice-cream van.

'Go and get two cornets, and a wafer for Mrs White,' ordered my mother, stuffing 10 shillings into my hand.

I ran off. I didn't know quite what fornicating was, but I had read about it in Deuteronomy, and I knew it was a sin. But why was it so noisy? Most sins you did quietly so as not to get caught. I bought the ice-creams and decided to take my time. When I got back my mother had opened the piano, and she and Mrs White were looking through the *Redemption Hymnal*.

I passed round the ice-creams.

'It's stopped,' I said brightly.

'For the moment,' said my mother grimly.

As soon as we had finished, my mother wiped her hands on her apron.

'*Ask the Saviour to Help You*, we'll sing that. Mrs White, you be the baritone.'

The first verse was very fine I thought:

'Yield not to Temptation, for yielding is sin,
Each Victory will help you some other to win.
Fight manfully onwards, Dark Passions subdue,
Look ever to Jesus, He will carry you through.'

The hymn had a rousing chorus that moved my mother to such an extent that she departed entirely from the notation of the *Redemption Hymnal*, and instead wrought her own huge chords that sounded the length of the piano. No note was exempt. By the time we got to verse 3, Next Door had started to bang on the wall.

'Listen to the Heathen,' my mother shouted jubilantly, her foot furious on the hard pedal.

'Sing it again.'

And we did, while the Heathen, driven mad by the Word, rushed away to find what blunt instruments they could to pound the wall from the other side.

Some of them ran into the back yard and yelled over the wall, 'Stop that bloody racket.'

'On a Sunday too,' tutted Mrs White, aghast.

My mother leapt from the keys and rushed into our back yard to quote the scripture. She found herself staring at the eldest son who had a lot of spots.

'The Lord help me,' she prayed, and a piece of Deuteronomy flashed into her mind:

'*The Lord will smite you with the boils of Egypt, and with the ulcers and the scurvey and the itch of which you cannot be cured.*' (Revised Standard Version.)

Then she ran back inside and slammed the back door.

'Now then,' she smiled, 'who's for a bit of dinner?'

My mother called herself a missionary on the home front. She said that the Lord hadn't called her to the hot places, like Pastor Spratt and his Glory Crusade, but to the streets and by-ways of Lancashire.

'I have always been guided by the Lord,' she told me. 'Look at my Wigan Work.'

A long time ago, very soon after her conversion, my mother had received a strange envelope, post marked Wigan. She had been suspicious, knowing how the Devil tempts the newly saved. The only person she knew in Wigan was an old flame, who had threatened to kill himself when she married another.

'That's up to you,' she had said, refusing to correspond.

Eventually curiosity got the upper hand, and she tore open the envelope. It wasn't from Pierre at all, but from one Eli Bone (Rev.) of the Society for the Lost.

The crest on the paper was a number of souls gathered round a mountain, with a little arch of a text underneath. '*Fastened to the Rock*', it said.

My mother read on . . .

Pastor Spratt, leaving Wigan on his way to Africa, had recommended my mother to the Society. They were looking for a new treasurer. The last, Mrs Maude Butler (née Richards), had just got married, and was moving to Morecambe. She would be opening a guest house for the bereaved, with special rates for all those who worked for the Society.

'A very attractive offer in itself,' reminded the Rev.

My mother was very flattered, and decided to accept the Rev.'s invitation to go and stay in Wigan for a few days, to find out more about the Society. My father was at work at the time, so she left him the address and a note which said: 'I am busy with the Lord in Wigan.'

She didn't come back for three weeks, and after that went regularly to the Rev. Bone's to audit the accounts and campaign for new members. She was a good business woman, and under her direction the Society for the Lost almost doubled in membership.

Every subscription form carried with it a number of tempting offers: discount on hymnbooks, and other religious accoutrements; a newsletter with a free gift every time, and a free record at Christmas; and, of course, the discounts available at the Morecambe guest house.

My mother regularly designed a gift of interest, available only to members of the Society. One year it was a fold-away, wipe-clean copy of Revelations, so that the blessed could be sure of the signs and portents surrounding the Second Coming. Another year, a Tribesman money box for missionary contributions. And my favourite of all, the sliding scale outdoor thermometer. On the one side of this sturdy Bakelite device was a simple temperature gauge, on the other, a sliding scale showing the number of possible conversions that could be made in a year, if every person, starting with you, brought two souls to the Lord. According to the sliding scale, the whole world could be godly within a mere ten years. This was a great encouragement to the timid and my mother received many letters of thanks.

The Society held a regular weekend at the Morecambe guest house, once a year, just before the busy season – the busy season being around Easter, after malingering illnesses contracted during the harsh winter. Of course, there was sometimes an unexpected spate in January, but it's surprising how long people hang on, once they know it's the end. My mother, who has always been interested in the End, personal and general, had a friend who used to make most of the wreaths for the Fylde coast.

'Our time's coming,' she used to say, every winter, and every winter she bought a new coat.

'It's the only time I can afford it,' she said. 'People live a lot longer now, and they don't want a fuss at the end.' She shook her head. 'No, business isn't what what it was.'

She used to come and stay with us sometimes, and bring her wires and sponges, and catalogues.

'It's funny, but they always want the same, never anything adventurous, although I once did a violin in carnations for a musician's husband.'

My mother nodded sympathetically.

The woman sipped her tea.

'Now, Queen Victoria, that was a funeral.'

She took a chocolate biscuit from the bottom of the pile.

'Course, I was young then, but my mother, she

wore her fingers to the bone making wreaths. And
they were wreaths in them days. Hearts and flowers,
coronets, family crests, look I still have them in my
catalogue.' She picked it up and showed us the faded
pages. 'But nobody wants 'em.'

She took another biscuit.

'Crosses,' she said bitterly, 'that's all I do, crosses. A
woman with my training it's not right.'

'Couldn't you do weddings as well?' I asked her.

'Weddings,' she spat, 'what would I want with
weddings?'

'You'd get a bit of variety,' I suggested.

'And what do you think they want at weddings?'
she challenged me.

I didn't know, I'd never been. Her eyes gleamed
down at me.

'Crosses,' she said, refilling her mug.

The weekend we all trouped down to Morecambe
for the Society spree, the woman was there as well.

'On contract work,' she told us.

Apparently there had been an epidemic at a nearby
boarding school. A lot of the pupils were no more,
and naturally their parents wanted wreaths.

'The school wants two tennis racquets in their
colours, as a tribute. I'm using mimosa and roses, it's
very difficult, but it's a challenge.'

'Well, the money won't go amiss, will it?' said my
mother.

'It'll pay for my bathroom that's what. A woman
of my training without a bathroom, it's shocking.'

I asked if I could help, and she said I could, so we
went down to the greenhouse together.

'Put these on.' She gave me a pair of gloves with no fingers. 'And start sorting them roses.'

Her own hands were red, and speckled with mimosa dust.

'What d'y think your mother would like?' she asked me, by way of conversation.

'Oh something very grand I think. I think she'd like the Bible open at Revelation.'

'Well, we'll see,' said the woman.

The woman and I got on very well. Years later, when I was needing a Saturday job, she helped me out. She had gone into partnership with an undertaker, so they could offer the whole package at special rates.

'It's a cut-throat business,' she told me.

They got a lot of work between them, and usually needed an extra hand. I went along to help with the laying out and make up. At first I was very clumsy. I used too much rouge, and smeared it down the cheekbones.

'Show some respect,' said the woman, 'the dead have their pride.' We always had a check list with the burial instructions, and soon this became my particular task. I went round making sure that the dead had everything they wanted. Some just asked for a prayer book or their Bible, or their wedding ring, but some were positively Egyptian. We did photograph albums, best dresses, favourite novels, and once someone's own novel. It was about a week in a telephone box with a pair of pyjamas called Adolf Hitler. The heroine was a piece of string with a knot in it.

'Some folk,' said the woman, when she read it.

But we put it in anyway. It reminded me of Rossetti who flung his new poems into the grave of his wife,

and had to ask permission from the home secretary
to get them out again six years later. I liked my work.
I learned a lot about wood and flowers, and I enjoyed
polishing the handles as a final touch.

'Always the best,' declared the woman.

One year, the Society had a special conference in
our town. My mother campaigned for weeks to make
sure we got a good turn-out. May and Alice went
posting invitations through letter boxes and Miss
Jewsbury was billed to play the oboe. It was an open
meeting to inform and encourage new members. The
only place we could find to host the meeting was the
Rechabite Hall on the corner of Infant Street.

'Do you think that's all right?' asked May anxiously.

'We won't look too deep,' replied my mother.

'But are they holy?' insisted Mrs White.

'That's for the Lord to decide,' my mother said,
very firm. Mrs White blushed, and later we saw she'd
taken her name off the volunteer list for buns.

The conference was booked for a Saturday, and there
was always a market near Infant Street on Saturdays,
so my mother gave me an orange box, and told me
to shout at everyone what was happening. I had a bad
time. Most of the street traders told me I was in their
way, that they had paid to be there, that I hadn't, and
so on. I didn't mind the abuse, I was well used to it,
and never thought it personal, but it was raining and
I wanted to do a good job. Eventually Mrs Arkwright
from the Factory Bottoms shop took pity on me. She
had a stall at the weekend mostly with pet food though
she would advise on vermin if it was urgent.

'I like my little break,' she said.

She let me put my orange box inside the shelter

of her stall, so that I could give out tracts without getting too wet.

'Tha mother's mad, tha knows,' she kept saying.

She might have been right, but there was nothing I could do about it.

I was relieved when two o'clock came and I could go inside with the rest.

'How many tracts did you give out?' demanded my mother, who was hovering by the door.

'All of them.'

She softened. 'Good girl.'

Someone started playing the piano just then, so I hurried inside. It was very gloomy with lots of pictures of the apostles. The sermon was on perfection, and it was at this moment that I began to develop my first theological disagreement.

Perfection, the man said, was a thing to aspire to. It was the condition of the Godhead, it was the condition of the man before the Fall. It could only be truly realized in the next world, but we had a sense of it, a maddening, impossible sense, which was both a blessing and a curse.

'Perfection,' he announced, 'is flawlessness.'

Once upon a time, in the forest, lived a woman who was so beautiful that the mere sight of her healed the sick and gave a good omen to the crops.

She was very wise too, being well acquainted with the laws of physics and the nature of the universe. Her great delight was to spin, and to sing songs as she turned the wheel. Meanwhile, in a part of the forest that had become a town, a great prince roamed sadly along the corridors of his palace. He was considered by many to be a good prince, and a valuable leader. He was also quite pretty, though a little petulant at times.

As he walked, he spoke aloud to his faithful companion, an old goose.

'If only I could find a wife,' he sighed. 'How can I run this whole kingdom without a wife?'

'You could delegate?' suggested the goose, waddling beside as best she could.

'Don't be silly,' snapped the prince. 'I'm a real prince.'

The goose blushed.

'The problem is,' continued the prince, 'there's a lot of girls, but no one who's got that special something.'

'What's that then?' panted the goose.

The prince gazed into space for a moment, then flung his body to the turf.

'Your hose has split, sire,' hissed his companion, embarrassed.

But the prince took no notice.

'That special something . . .' He rolled over, and propped himself on an elbow, motioning the goose to do the same.

'I want a woman, without blemish inside or out, flawless in every respect. I want a woman who is perfect.'

And he buried his face in the grass and began to cry.

The goose was much moved by this display, and shuffled off to see if she could find some advisors.

After a long search, she stumbled on a clump of them under the royal oaks, playing bridge.

'The prince wants a wife.'

They looked up as one man.

'The prince wants a wife,' she repeated, 'and she

must be without blemish inside or out, flawless in every respect. She must be perfect.'

The youngest advisor got out his bugle horn and sounded the cry. 'For a wife,' he shouted. 'Perfect.'

For three years the advisors roamed the land to no avail. They found many lovely and virtuous women, but the prince refused them all.

'Prince, you're a fool,' said the goose one day. 'What you want can't exist.'

'It must exist,' insisted the prince, 'because I want it.'

'You'll die first,' shrugged the goose, about to go back to her feeding tray.

'Not before you,' spat the prince, and chopped off her head.

Three more years passed, and the prince began to write a book to pass the time. It was called *The Holy Mystery of Perfection*. He divided it into three sections.

Part one: the philosophy of perfection. The Holy Grail, the unblemished life, the final aspiration on Mount Carmel. Saint Teresa and the Interior Castle.

Part two: the impossibility of perfection. The restless search in this life, the pain, the majority who opt for second best. Their spreading corruption. The importance of being earnest.

Part three: the need to produce a world full of perfect beings. The possibility thereby of a heaven on earth. A perfect race. An exhortation to single-mindedness.

The prince was very pleased with his book, and had a copy given to all his advisors, so that they should not waste his time with the merely second-best. One of them took it with him to a distant corner of the forest, where he could read in peace. He wasn't academic, and the prince had a very dense prose style.

While he was lying under a tree, he heard the sound of singing coming from somewhere on the left. Curious, and a music lover, he got up to find out who was making the noise. In a clearing, there was a woman spinning thread and accompanying herself with a song.

The advisor thought she was the most beautiful thing he had ever seen.

'And she can sew,' he thought.

He went up to her, bowing as he came.

'Fair maid,' he began.

'If you want to chat,' she said, 'you'll have to come back later, I'm working to a deadline.'

The advisor was very shocked.

'But I am royal,' he told her.

'And I'm working to a deadline,' she told him. 'Come for lunch if you want.'

'I'll be back at noon,' he answered stiffly and marched off.

Meantime, the advisor questioned whoever he met about the woman. How old was she? Who were her family? Did she have any dependants? Was she clever?

'Clever?' snorted one old man. 'She's perfect.'

'Did you say perfect?' urged the advisor, shaking the old man by the shoulders.

'Yes,' cried he, 'I said perfect.'

As soon as it was noon the advisor banged on the door of the woman's home.

'It's cheese soup,' she said, as she let him in.

'Never mind that,' he retorted, 'we've got to get moving, I'm taking you to the prince.'

'What for?' asked the woman, ladling out her own soup.

'He might want to marry you,'

'I'm not getting married,' she said.

The advisor turned to her in horror. 'Why not?'

'It's not something I'm very interested in. Now do you want this soup or don't you?'

'No,' shouted the young man. 'But I'll be back.'

Three days later, there was a great commotion in the forest. The prince and his retinue were arriving. The prince himself had lost the use of his legs from sitting still so long, and had to be carried in a litter. At the sight of the woman, who was sitting spinning, just as before, he leapt from his pallet, crying, 'I'm cured, she must be perfect.' And he fell on his knees and begged her to marry him.

The court turned to one another, smiling. They could stop all this nonsense now, and live happily ever after.

The woman smiled down on the kneeling price and stroked his hair.

'You're very sweet, but I don't want to marry you.'

There was a gasp of horror from the gathered court. Then silence.

The prince struggled to his feet, and pulled a copy of his book from out of his pocket.

'But you must, I've written all about you.'

Again the woman smiled, and read the title. Then she frowned, and motioning to the prince, pulled him inside her home.

For three days and three nights the court camped in fear. No sound came from the hut. Then on the fourth day, the prince appeared, weary and unwashed.

Calling his chief advisors around him, he told them all that had taken place.

The woman was indeed perfect, there was no doubt about that, but she wasn't flawless. He, the prince, had been wrong. She was perfect because she was a perfect balance of qualities and strengths. She was symmetrical in every respect. The search for perfection, she had told him, was in fact the search for balance, for harmony. And she showed him Libra, the scales, and Pisces, the fish, and last of all put out her two hands. 'Here is the clue,' she said. 'Here in this first and personal balance.'

'There are two principles,' she said, 'the Weight and the Counter-weight.'

'Oh yes,' put in one of the advisors, 'you mean the sphere of Destiny and the wheel of Fortune.'

The prince swivelled round.

'How do you know?' he demanded.

The advisor blushed. 'Oh, it's just something my mother told me, I'd forgotten it until now.'

'Well anyway,' said the prince peremptorily, 'the point is I'm wrong and I'm going to have to write a new book, and make a public apology to the goose.'

'Sire, you cannot,' gasped the advisors, as one man.

'Why not?'

'Because you are a prince, and as a prince you cannot be seen to be wrong.'

That night the prince paced the forest, hoping to find a solution. On the stroke of midnight he heard a sound behind him, and drawing his sword came face to face with his chief advisor.

'Lucien,' he exclaimed (for it was he).

'Sire,' the man answered, bowing deeply. 'I have a

solution.' And for forty-five minutes he whispered in the prince's ear.

'No,' cried the prince, 'I cannot.'

'Sire, you must, your kingdom is at stake.'

'No one will believe me,' wept the prince, sitting on a log.

'They will, they must, they always do,' replied his advisor evenly. 'Trust me.'

'Must I?' asked the prince wildly.

'You must,' said the advisor, very firm.

The night continued, and the prince fixed his heart to evil. At dawn, there was a great trumpet cry, and all the court and all the village assembled together to hear what the prince had to say.

He stood in their midst, newly washed, and called for the woman to come forth.

As she came from her home, the first light caught her, and she shone beacon-like across the clearing. There was a murmur of amazement, for she was more beautiful than ever that day. The prince swallowed hard, and began his speech.

'Good people, all of you know of my search for perfection, and many of you I hope have read my book. I had hoped on coming here to find an end to my quest, but I now know that perfection is not to be found, but to be fashioned, there is no such thing as flawlessness on this earth . . .'

'But there is such a thing as perfection,' the woman spoke out, her voice clear and strong.

'This woman,' continued the prince, 'has done her best to convince me that perfection and flawlessness are not the same thing, and why should she take such trouble if she were not flawed herself?'

'I took no trouble,' returned the woman, as strong as before. 'It was you who sought me.'

There was a ripple of dissent among the crowd. Suddenly someone cried out.

'But she healed you!'

'Heathen arts,' snapped back the chief advisor. 'Arrest that man.' And the man was bound, and taken away.

'But she has no blemish,' shouted out another.

'But I have,' said the woman quietly, 'I have many.'

'Proof from her own lips,' screamed the chief advisor.

Then the woman took a step forward and stood before the prince who began to tremble uncontrollably.

'What you want does not exist,' she said.

'Proof from her own lips,' screamed the chief advisor again.

The woman took no notice, but continued to address the prince, who had turned deathly pale.

'What does exist lies in the sphere of your own hands.'

The prince fainted.

'Evil, Evil,' shrieked the advisor. 'We will not give up on our task.'

'You'll be dead first,' shrugged the woman, about to go back inside.

'Not before you,' cried the prince, coming to. 'Off with her head.'

And they chopped off the woman's head.

Instantly, the blood became a lake, and drowned the advisors and most of the court. The prince only managed to escape by climbing a tree.

'This is a tedious affair,' he thought. 'Still, at least I have stamped out a very great evil. Now I must continue my quest, but alas, who will ever advise me?'

At that moment, he heard a noise beneath him. He looked down, and saw a man selling oranges.

'What a good idea,' exclaimed the prince, 'I'll get a dozen for the trip home.'

'Old man,' he hailed, 'sell me a dozen oranges.'

The old man fumbled out a dozen, and put them into a bag.

'Got anything else?' asked the prince, feeling better.

'Sorry,' said the seller, 'I only does oranges.'

'Oh dear,' sighed the prince, 'I was hoping for something to read on the way back.'

The old man sniffed.

'No magazines?'

The old man shook his head.

'No informative booklets?'

The old man wiped his nose.

'Oh well, I'll go then,' decided the prince.

'Wait a minute,' said the man suddenly, 'I got this.'

And he pulled from his pocket a leather bound book. 'I don't know if it's up your street, it tells you how to build a perfect person, it's all about this man who does it, but it's no good if you ain't got the equipment.'

The prince snatched it away.

'It's a bit weird,' continues the old man, 'this geezer gets a bolt through the neck . . .'

But the prince had gone.

NUMBERS

IT WAS SPRING, the ground still had traces of snow, and I was about to be married. My dress was pure white and I had a golden crown. As I walked up the aisle the crown got heavier and heavier and the dress more and more difficult to walk in. I thought everyone would point at me, but no one noticed.

Somehow I made it to the altar. The priest was very fat and kept getting fatter, like bubble gum you blow. Finally we came to the moment, 'You may kiss the bride.' My new husband turned to me, and here were a number of possibilities. Sometimes he was blind, sometimes a pig, sometimes my mother, sometimes the man from the post office, and once, just a suit of clothes with nothing inside. I told my mother about it, and she said it was because I ate sardines for supper. The next night I ate sausages, but I still had the dream.

There was a woman in our street who told us all she had married a pig. I asked her why she did it, and she said 'You never know until it's too late.'

Exactly.

No doubt that woman had discovered in life what I had discovered in my dreams. She had unwittingly married a pig.

I kept watch on him after that. It was hard to tell he was a pig. He was clever, but his eyes were close together, and his skin bright pink. I tried to imagine him without his clothes on. Horrid.

Other men I knew weren't much better. The man who ran the post office was bald and shiny with hands too fat for the sweet jars. He called me poppet, which my mother said was nice. He gave me sweets too, which was an improvement.

One day he had a new sort.

'Sweet hearts for a sweet heart,' he said and laughed. That day I had almost strangled my dog with rage, and been dragged from the house by a desperate mother. Sweet I was not. But I was a little girl, ergo, I was sweet, and here were sweets to prove it. I looked in the bag. Yellow and pink and sky blue and orange, and all of them heart-shaped and all of them said things like,

Maureen 4 Ken

Jack' n' Jill, True.

On the way home I crunched at the *Maureen 4 Ken's*. I was confused. Everyone always said you found the right man.

My mother said it, which was confusing.

My auntie said it, which was even more confusing.

The man in the post office sold it on sweets.

But there was the problem of the woman married to the pig, and the spotty boy who took girls down backs, and my dream.

That afternoon I went to the library. I went the long way, so as to miss the couples. They made funny noises that sounded painful, and the girls were always squashed against the wall. In the library I felt better, words you could trust and look at till you understood them, they couldn't change half way through a sentence like people, so it was easier to spot a lie. I found a book of fairy tales, and read one called 'Beauty and the Beast.'

In this story, a beautiful young woman finds herself the forfeit of a bad bargain made by her father. As a result, she has to marry an ugly beast, or dishonour her family forever. Because she is good, she obeys. On her wedding night, she gets into bed with the beast, and feeling pity that everything should be so ugly, gives it a little kiss. Immediately, the beast is transformed into a handsome young prince, and they both live happily every after.

I wondered if the woman married to a pig had read this story. She must have been awfully disappointed if she had. And what about my Uncle Bill, he was horrible, and hairy, and looking at the picture, transformed princes aren't meant to be hairy at all.

Slowly I closed the book. It was clear that I had stumbled on a terrible conspiracy.

There are women in the world.

There are men in the world.

And there are beasts.

What do you do if you marry a beast?

Kissing them didn't always help.

And beasts are crafty. They disguise themselves like you and I.

Like the wolf in 'Little Red Riding Hood'.

Why had no one told me? Did that mean no one else knew?

Did that mean that all over the globe, in all innocence, women were marrying beasts?

I reassured myself as best I could. The minister was a man, but he wore a skirt, so that made him special. There must be others, but were there enough? That was the worry. There were a lot of women, and most of them got married: If they couldn't marry each other, and I didn't think they could, because of having babies, some of them would inevitably have to marry beasts.

My own family had done quite badly, I thought.

If only there was some way of telling, then we could operate a ration system. It wasn't fair that a whole street should be full of beasts.

That night, we had to go to my auntie's to play Beetle. She was in the team at church, and needed to practise. As she dealt the cards, I asked her, 'Why are so many men really beasts?'

She laughed. 'You're too young for that.'

My uncle had overheard. He came over to me, and put his face close.

'You wouldn't love us any other way,' he said, and rubbed his spiky chin against my face. I hated him.

'Leave off Bill,' my auntie pushed him away. 'Don't worry love,' she soothed, 'you'll get used to it. When I married, I laughed for a week, cried for a month, and settled down for life. It's different, that's all, they have their little ways.' I looked at my uncle who was now sunk in the pools coupon.

'You hurt me,' I accused.

'No I didn't,' he grinned. 'It was just a bit of love.'

'That's what you always say,' my auntie retorted, 'now shut up or go out.'

He slunk off. I half expected him to have a tail.

She spread the cards. 'There's time enough for you to get a boy.'

'I don't think I want one.'

'There's what we want,' she said, putting down a jack, 'and there's what we get, remember that.'

Was she trying to tell me she knew about the beasts? I got very depressed and started putting the Beetle legs on the wrong way round, and generally making a mess. Eventually my auntie stood up and sighed. 'You might as well go home,' she said.

I went to fetch my mother who was in the parlour listening to Johnny Cash.

'Come on, we're finished.'

Slowly she put on her coat, and picked up her little Bible, the travel size one. We set off together down the street.

'I've got to talk to you, have you got time?'

'Yes,' she said, 'let's have an orange.'

I tried to explain my dream, and the beast theory, and how much I hated Uncle Bill. All the time my mother walked along humming *What a Friend We Have in Jesus*, and peeling me an orange. She stopped peeling and I stopped talking about the same time. I had one last question.

'Why did you marry my dad?'

She looked at me closely.

'Don't be silly.'

'I'm not being silly.'

'We had to have something for you, and besides, he's a good man, though I know he's not one to push himself. But don't you worry, you're dedicated to the Lord, I put you down for missionary school as soon as we got you. Remember Jane Eyre and St John Rivers.' A faraway look came into her eye.

I did remember, but what my mother didn't know was that I now knew she had rewritten the ending.

Jane Eyre was her favourite non-Bible book, and she read it to me over and over again, when I was very small. I couldn't read it, but I knew where the pages turned. Later, literate and curious, I had decided to read it for myself. A sort of nostalgic pilgrimage. I found out, that dreadful day in a back corner of the library, that Jane doesn't marry St John at all, that she goes back to Mr Rochester. It was like the day I discovered my adoption papers while searching for a pack of playing cards. I have never since played cards, and I have never since read *Jane Eyre*.

We continued our walk in silence. She thought I was satisfied, but I was wondering about her, and wondering where I would go to find out what I wanted to know.

When it was washday I hid in the dustbin to hear what the women said. Nellie came out with her bit of rope and strung it up nail to nail across the back alley. She waved to Doreen who was struggling up the hill with her shopping, offering her a cup of tea and a talk. Each Wednesday Doreen queued up at the butcher's for the special offer mince. It always put her in a bad mood because she was a member of the Labour party and believed in equal shares and equal rights. She started to tell Nellie about the woman in front buying steak. Nellie shook her head which was small and tufted, and said it had been hard for her too since Bert died.

'Bert,' spat Doreen, 'he were dead ten years before they laid him out.' Then she offered Nellie a wine gum.

'Well I don't like to speak ill of the dead,' said Nellie uneasily, 'you never know.'

Doreen snorted and squatted painfully on the back step. Her skirt was too tight, but she always pretended it had shrunk.

'What about speaking ill of the living? My Frank's up to no good.'

Nellie took a deep breath and another wine gum. She asked if it was the woman who served pie and peas in the pub; Doreen didn't know, but now that she thought of it that would explain why he always smelled of gravy when he came home late.

'You should never have married him,' scolded Nellie.

'I didn't know what he was when I married him did I?' And she told Nellie about the war and how her dad had liked him, and how it seemed sensible. 'I should have guessed though, what kind of a man comes round to court you and ends up drinking with your dad instead? I used to sit all done up playing whist with his mother and one of her friends.'

'Did he not take you anywhere then?'

'Oh yes,' said Doreen, 'we used to go down the dog track every Saturday afternoon.'

The two of them sat in silence for a while then Doreen went on, 'Course the children helped. I ignored him for fifteen years.'

'Still,' Nellie reassured her, 'you're not as bad as Hilda across the road, her one drinks every penny, and she daren't go to the police.'

'If mine touched me I'd have him put away,' said Doreen grimly.

'Would you?'

Doreen paused and scratched in the dirt with her shoe.

'Let's have a smoke,' offered Nellie, 'and you tell me about Jane.'

Jane was Doreen's daughter, just turned seventeen and very studious.

'If she don't get a boyfriend folks will talk. She spends all her time at that Susan's doing her homework, or so she tells me.'

Nellie thought that Jane might be seeing a boy on the quiet, pretending to be at Susan's. Doreen shook her head. 'She's there all right, I check with Susan's mother. If they're not careful folk will think they're like them two at the paper shop.'

'I like them two,' said Nellie firmly, 'and who's to say they do anything?'

'Mrs Fergeson across saw them getting a new bed, a double bed.'

'Well what does that prove? Me and Bert had one bed but we did nothing in it.'

Doreen said that was all very well, but two women were different.

Different from what? I wondered from inside the dustbin.

'Well your Jane can go to university and move away, she's clever.'

'Frank won't put up with that, he wants grandchildren, and if I don't get a move on there'll be no dinner for him and he'll be back with pie and peas in the pub. I don't want to give him an excuse.'

She struggled to her feet as Nellie started to peg out the washing. When it was safe, I crept out of the dustbin, as confused as ever and covered in soot.

It was a good thing I was destined to become a missionary. For some time after this I put aside the problem of men and concentrated on reading the Bible. Eventually, I thought, I'll fall in love like everybody else. Then some years later, quite by mistake, I did.

My mother said that we had to go down town.

'I'm not coming.'

'Get that mac on.'

'I'm not coming, it's raining.'

'I know and I'm not going to get wet on my own.' She threw that mac at me and turned to the mirror to adjust her headscarf. I kicked the dog out of her box, and tried to clip on her lead. My mother spied me. 'Leave that thing, it'll only get trodden on.'

'But . . .'

'*Leave it*!' And she grabbed her shopping bag in one hand and me in the other and dragged me off to the bus, complaining all the way about ingratitude. When we got on the bus we saw May with Ida, one of the women who ran the forbidden paper shop, and played bowls for the local team.

'Look out, it's Louie with the nipper,' hailed May with pleasure.

'No nipper now,' said Ida, 'she's fourteen if she's a day. Have one of these coconut macaroons.' And she stuck out a crumpled bag.

'Thanks,' said my mother, and took one.

'Art going down town?' asked May.

My mother nodded.

'Well I tell you, there's nowt that's cheap if you want fruit, only some muck from Spain.'

'We're getting mince,' said my mother, folding herself round her handbag. She didn't like talking about money.

'Well I tell you, there's nowt,' repeated May. 'I tell

you what though.' She leaned forward, pinning my hair to the seat with her bosom.

'May,' I gasped.

'Auntie May,' snapped my mother.

'Let's meet up at Trickett's for a cup of Horlicks at three o'clock.' And she leaned back, pleased, letting free my scalp.

'Look, Louie, that child's moulting.' May poked my mother and waved the strands of my hair attached to her coat.

'They do at that age,' Ida butted in. 'It's nowt.'

The bus pulled into the Boulevard. (My mother always called it that because of her memories of Paris.) May and Ida went off to the tripe stall, and my mother went into the newsagent's, only to find they had forgotten to save her *Band of Hope* review. I was foolish enough to ask if I could have a new mac.

'That mac'll outlast your father,' was the retort.

We went into the market next. My mother always got her mince cheap because the butcher had been her sweetheart once. She said he was a devil, but she still took the mince. While he was wrapping it up, I got my mac caught on a meat hook and pulled the sleeve off.

'Mum,' I wailed, waving it at her.

'Beezum,' she cried. And she took out a roll of sellotape and started to wind it round my arm. At that moment we saw Mrs Clifton, who gave singing lessons, and did her shopping at Marks and Spencers.

'Is something the matter with Jeanette's arm?' she enquired.

'It's just her sleeve,' replied my mother, keeping her 'h' as best she could.

'Oh, but I think she needs a new one, don't you?'

My mother shifted her shopping bag.

'No I don't,' I piped up, 'I really like this one.'

She looked at me with distaste.

'Well, I do think . . .'

'We're getting a new one this afternoon,' said my mother firmly. 'Goodbye.' She moved us away, leaving Mrs Clifton alone beside the belly of pork.

'You're a disgrace,' hissed my mother, as soon as she could. 'What would your grandad say?'

'He's dead.'

'That's not the point.'

'She's stuck up and I don't like her.'

'You be quiet, she has a lovely home.'

Before I could protest any further she pushed me inside a shop that sold oddments and seconds.

'They haven't got any,' I said, peering about with some relief.

'Oh yes they have,' answered my mother triumphantly.

She was rummaging behind a pile of cardboard boxes that had SURPLUS written on the side, like branded sheep.

'Try this one.'

I put it on.

It was enormous.

'Look, it's got a hat with it.'

She thrust a shapeless piece of plastic towards the place she thought my hand would be.

'Which way round does it go?' I was feeling trapped.

'It'll keep you dry which ever way.'

I remembered a film I had seen called *The Man in the Iron Mask*.

'It's a bit big,' I ventured.

'You can grow into it.'

'But Mum . . .'

'We'll have it.'

'But Mum.'

It was bright pink.

We walked in silence to the fish stall.

I hated her.

I looked at the shrimps.

They were pink all over too.

There was a woman next to me carrying a Battenburg cake.

It had pink icing and little pink roses.

I felt sick.

Then somebody was sick. A small boy. His mother hit him.

'Serve him right,' I thought meanly.

I wondered whether to drop my hat in it, but I knew she'd make me wear it just the same.

I felt miserable. When Keats felt miserable he always put on a clean shirt.

But he was a poet.

I wouldn't have noticed Melanie if I hadn't gone round the other side of the stall to look at the aquarium.

She was boning kippers on a big marble slab. She used a thin stained knife, and threw the gut into a tin bucket. The clean fish she laid on greaseproof paper, and every fourth fish had a sprig of parsley.

'I'd like to do that,' I said.

She smiled and carried on.

'Do you like doing it?'

Still she said nothing, so I slid, as discreetly as a person in a pink plastic mac can, to the other side of the tank. I couldn't see very well because of the hood over my eyes.

'Can I have some fish-bait?' I asked.

She looked up, and I noticed her eyes were a lovely grey, like the cat Next Door.

'I'm not supposed to have friends at work.'

'But I'm not your friend,' I pointed out, rudely.

'No, but they'll think you are,' she replied.

'Well I might as well be then,' I suggested.

She stared at me a moment, then turned away.

'Get a move on,' hastened my mother, suddenly appearing round the whelk tray.

'Can I have a new fish for my tank?'

'We've hardly enough money to feed what we have got, without another mouth. That damn dog costs enough.'

'Only a small one, a fantail?'

'I've said no.' And she marched off towards Trickett's.

I felt wronged. If she had taught me to read like other children had been taught to read, I wouldn't have these obsessions. I'd be happy with a pet rabbit and the odd stick insect.

I looked behind me.

But Melanie had gone.

When we got to Trickett's, May and Ida were already there. Ida was doing her pools coupon and eating raspberry ripple.

'Look out, it's them,' she nudged May as we came in.

My mother sank down.

'I'm finished.'

'Get some Horlicks down,' May shouted for the waitress, who put down her cigarette and sloped across.

Her glasses were at a funny angle, and stuck together with band-aid.

'What you done?' demanded May, 'You weren't like that just now.'

'That Mona put her new delivery of beefburgers on them,' she answered peevishly, easing herself against the wall.

'They freeze them just like bricks nowadays.'

She flicked a dishcloth over the table.

'Just like bricks, it's not natural.'

She wiped out the ashtray.

'Not that I think there's owt wrong with a fridge mind, but you can go too far.'

'You can,' agreed May. 'You can.'

'I had that Mrs Clifton in here this morning,' the waitress went on. 'She's a right one, common as muck, but all fancy with it.' (My mother blushed.)

'I said to her, I said, Doreen, what you pay at Marks and Sparks you get for half the price down here.'

Ida murmured her assent.

'But you know what she said back?'

May said she didn't but she could guess.

'She said, posh as anything, I like to fill my freezer with things I know are good, Mrs Grimsditch.'

'Ho, she's a one,' exclaimed May. 'Called you Mrs Grimsditch did she? What's wrong with Betty then?'

'Aye,' put in Ida, 'what's wrong with Betty?'

And they all started chorusing under their breath.

My mother was getting desperate.

'Mrs Grimsditch . . .' she began.

'What's wrong with Betty?' glowered the waitress, turning round.

My mother turned to Ida for some help, but Ida was busy with her coupon.

'Liverpool against the Rovers,' she said to May. 'What do you reckon?'

'Nowt,' said Betty, butting in. 'Now what do you want? I haven't got all day, there'll all them glasses to wash.'

My mother was visibly distressed.

'People spit in them and all sorts, it's enough to turn your stomach.'

She looked at me.

'Do you want a Saturday job?'

My mother brightened up.

'Yes she does.'

'Well it can start now, can't it Betty?' Ida spoke from behind her pools coupon.

'Aye,' said Betty, 'there's all them glasses.'

So I set to work, while my mother and Ida and May filled in the coupon and drank Horlicks. I didn't mind the work, and there wasn't much spit in the glasses, besides it gave me time to think about the fish stall, and Melanie.

Week after week I went back there, just to watch.

Then one week she wasn't there any more.

There was nothing I could do but stare and stare at the whelks.

Whelks are strange and comforting.

They have no notion of community life and they breed very quietly.

But they have a strong sense of personal dignity.

Even lying face down in a tray of vinegar, there is something noble about a whelk.

Which cannot be said for everybody.

'Why do I feel like this?' I wondered. Then, just as I was about to turn away and buy myself a baked potato for comfort, I saw Melanie walking round to the stall. I went straight up to her. She looked a bit surprised.

'Hello, I thought you'd left.'

'I have left, I've got a job in the library now, just Saturday mornings.'

What could I say next? How could I make her stay?

'Would you like a baked potato?' I offered wildly.

She smiled, and said she would and we went to eat it on the bench outside Woolworth's. I was very nervous, and the pigeons got most of mine. She talked about the weather and her mother, that she had no father. 'I haven't either,' I said, to make her feel better. 'Well, not much.' Then I had to explain about our church and my mother and me being dedicated to the Lord. It sounded odd for a moment, but I knew that was because I felt nervous. I asked her if she went to church, and she said she did, but not a very lively one, so of course I invited her to ours the next day.

'Melanie,' I plucked up courage to ask at last, 'why do you have such a funny name?'

She blushed. 'When I was born I looked like a melon.'

'Don't worry,' I reassured her, 'you don't any more.'

The first time that Melanie came to our church was not a success. I'd forgotten that Pastor Finch was visiting on his regional tour. He arrived in an old Bedford van with the terrified damned painted on one side and the heavenly host painted on the other. On the back doors and front bonnet he'd inscribed in green lettering, HEAVEN OR HELL? IT'S

YOUR CHOICE. He was very proud of the bus, and told of the many miracles worked inside and out. Inside had six seats, so that the choir could travel with him, leaving enough room for musical instruments and a large first-aid kit in case the demon combusted somebody.

'What do you do about the flames?' we asked.

'I use an extinguisher,' he explained.

We were very impressed.

There was a collapsible cross that fitted across the back doors, and a very small sink so that the pastor could wash his hands after every operation.

'Water is of the essence,' he reminded us, 'just as Christ bade the swine leap into the sea, so I rinse the demon under this tap.'

After we had all admired the bus for long enough, Pastor Finch led us back into the church and asked his choir to sing his latest composition. 'It came to me from the Lord, just as I left Sandbach Motorway Services.' The song was called *You Don't Need Spirits When You've Got the Spirit*. The first verse went like this . . .

> *'Some men turn to whisky, some women turn to gin,*
> *But there ain't no better rapture than drinking the spirit in.*
> *Some men like their beer, others like their wine,*
> *But open your mouth to the Spirit, if you want to feel fine.'*

The choir sang this and the rest of the verses, six in all, and we had a sheet to join in the chorus, which was accompanied by Pastor Finch on the bongos.

The chorus went like this . . .

> *'Not whisky rye not gin and dry not rum and coke for*
> *me.*
> *Not brandy fizz but a Spiritual whizz puts the fire in*
> *me.'*

We had a wonderful time. Danny got out his guitar and picked up the chords, then May started beating out that twelve-bar on her tambourine. Before long we were all in a long line going clockwise round the church singing the chorus over and over again.

'The Lord is working mightily,' puffed Pastor Finch, smacking the bongos with his palms. 'Praise the Lord.'

'Roy, don't tax yourself so,' fussed Mrs Finch who was desperately trying to keep up on the piano. 'Somebody take those bongos off him.' But nobody did, and it wasn't until Mrs Rothwell fell over that we finally stopped.

It was only then that I noticed that Melanie hadn't joined in.

'Now for the sermon,' shouted Pastor Finch, and we all settled back to enjoy ourselves. He told us about the doings of his tour, how many souls had been saved, how many good souls, oppressed by the demon, had found peace once again.

'I'm not one to boast,' he reminded us, 'but the Lord has given me a mighty gift.' We murmured our agreement. Then we were shocked as he described the epidemic of demons, even now spreading through the north west. Lancashire and Cheshire had been particular blighted; only the day before he had cleansed a whole family in Cheadle Hulme.

'Ridden they were.' His eyes roamed the hushed congregation. 'Yes, ridden, and do you know why?'

He took a step back. We didn't make a sound. 'Unnatural Passions.'

A tremor shook the gathering. Not all of us were sure what he meant, but all of us knew it was dreadful. I glanced across at Melanie; she looked like she was going to be sick.

'Must be the Spirit,' I thought, and gave her hand a little squeeze. She jumped, and stared at me. Yes, definitely the Spirit.

At the end of his very fine sermon, Pastor Finch made an appeal, he urged any sinner to raise their hand, and ask forgiveness there and then. We bowed our heads in prayer, squinting up now and again, to see if it was working. Suddenly, I felt a hand on mine. It was Melanie.

'I am going to do it,' she hissed, and pushed her other arm into the air.

'Yes, I see your hand,' acknowledged Pastor Finch.

A ripple of joy ran through the church. There was no one else, so Melanie had plenty of attention at the end of the service. Not that she wanted it. 'I feel terrible,' she confided.

'Don't worry,' breezed Alice, who was passing by, 'It's homeopathic.'

Poor Melanie, she didn't understand any of them, she just knew she needed Jesus. Then she asked me to be her counsellor, and I agreed to go round to her house every Monday, while her mum was at the club where she worked. We left together, me on a cloud, and her with a handbag full of tracts on the gifts of the Spirit, and advice for new converts. As we reached the town hall, Pastor Finch shot past us, his gospel radio full on, windows wide open, and on the top of the van, a flag flying triumphant.

'That's his Salvation Flag,' I told Melanie. 'Whenever someone gets saved he hoists it up.'

'Let's get on the bus,' she replied, a bit desperate.

So each Monday after that I went round to Melanie's and we read the Bible together, and usually spent half an hour in prayer. I was delighted. She was my friend, and I wasn't used to that, apart from Elsie. Somehow, this was different. I talked about her all the time at home, and my mother never responded. Then one day she bundled me into the kitchen and said we had to talk seriously.

'There's a boy at church I think you're keen on.'

'What?' I said, completely mystified.

She meant Graham, a newish convert, who'd moved over to our town from Stockport. I was teaching him to play the guitar, and trying to make him understand the importance of regular Bible study.

'It's time,' she went on, very solemn, 'that I told you about Pierre and how I nearly came to a bad end.' Then she poured us both a cup of tea and opened a packet of Royal Scot. I was enthralled.

'It's not something I'm proud of, and I'll only say it once.'

My mother had been headstrong, and had got a job teaching in Paris, which was a very daring thing to do at the time. She had lived off the Rue St Germain, eaten croissants and lived a clean life. She wasn't with the Lord then, but she had high standards. Then, one sunny day, without warning, she had been walking towards the river when she met Pierre, or rather Pierre had jumped from his bicycle, offered her his onions, and named her the most beautiful woman he had ever seen.

'Naturally, I was flattered.'

They exchanged addresses, and began to court one another. It was then that my mother experienced a feeling she had never known before: a fizzing and a buzzing and a certain giddiness. Not only with Pierre, but anywhere, at any time.

'Well, I thought it must be love.'

But this puzzled her because Pierre wasn't very clever, and didn't have much to say, except to exclaim how beautiful she was. Perhaps he was handsome? But no, looking in the magazines, she realised he wasn't that either. But the feeling wouldn't go away. Then, on a quiet night, after a quiet supper, Pierre had seized her and begged her to stay with him that night. The fizzing began, and as he clutched her to him, she felt sure she would never love another, and yes she would stay and after that, they would marry.

'Lord forgive me, but I did it.'

My mother stopped, overcome with emotion. I begged her to finish the story, proffering the Royal Scots.

'The worst is still to come.'

I speculated on the worst, while she chewed her biscuit. Perhaps I wasn't a child of God at all, but the daughter of a Frenchman.

A couple of days afterward, my mother had gone to see the doctor in a fit of guilty anxiety. She lay on the couch while the doctor prodded her stomach and chest, asking if she ever felt giddy, or fizzy in the belly. My mother coyly explained that she was in love, and that she often felt strange, but that wasn't the reason for her visit.

'You may well be in love,' said the doctor, 'but you also have a stomach ulcer.'

Imagine my mother's horror. She had given away

her all for an ailment. She took the tablets, followed the diet, and refused Pierre's entreaties to visit her. Needless to say, the next time they met, and again by chance, she felt nothing, nothing at all, and shortly fled the country to avoid him.

'Then am I . . . ?' I began.

'There was no issue,' she said quickly.

For a few moments we sat silent, then:

'So just you take care, what you think is the heart might well be another organ.'

It might, mother, it might, I thought. She got up and told me to go and find something to do. I decided to go and see Melanie, but just as I reached the door she called me back with a word of warning.

'Don't let anyone touch you Down There,' and she pointed to somewhere at the level of her apron pocket.

'No Mother,' I said meekly, and fled.

When I reached Melanie's it was getting dark. I had to cut through the churchyard to get there, and sometimes I'd steal her a bunch of flowers from the new graves. She was always pleased, but then, I never told her where they came from. She asked me if I wanted to stay overnight because her mum was away and she didn't like being in the house on her own. I said I'd ring a neighbour, and after much trouble finally got an agreement from my mother, who had to be fetched from her lettuces. We read the Bible as usual, and then told each other how glad we were that the Lord had brought us together. She stroked my head for a long time, and then we hugged and it felt like drowning. Then I was frightened but couldn't stop. There was something crawling in my belly. I had an octopus inside me.

And it was evening and it was morning; another day.

After that we did everything together, and I stayed with her as often as I could. My mother seemed relieved that I was seeing less of Graham, and for a while made no mention of the amount of time I spent with Melanie.

'Do you think this is Unnatural Passion?' I asked her once.

'Doesn't feel like it. According to Pastor Finch, that's awful.' She must be right, I thought.

Melanie and I had volunteered to set up the Harvest Festival Banquet, and we worked hard in the church throughout the day. When everyone arrived and started to pass the potato pie, we stood on the balcony, looking down on them. Our family. It was safe.

Here is a table set at feast, and the guests are arguing about the best recipe for goose. Now and again a tremour shakes the chandelier, dropping tiny flakes of plaster into the sherbet. The guests look up more in interest than alarm. It's cold in here, very cold. The women suffer most. Their shoulders bared and white like hard-boiled eggs. Outside, under the snow, the river lies embalmed. These are the elect, and in the hall an army sleeps on straw.

Outside a rush of torches.

Laughter drifts into the hall. The elect have always been this way.

Getting old, dying, starting again. Not noticing.

Father and Son. Father and Son.

It has always been this way, nothing can intrude.

Father Son and Holy Ghost.

Outside, the rebels storm the Winter Palace.

DEUTERONOMY
The last book of the law

TIME IS A great deadener. People forget, get bored, grow old, go away. There was a time in England when everyone was much concerned with building wooden boats and sailing off against the Turk. When that stopped being interesting, what peasants there were left limped back to the land, and what nobles there were left plotted against each other.

Of course that is not the whole story, but that is the way with stories; we make them what we will. It's a way of explaining the universe while leaving the universe unexplained, it's a way of keeping it all alive, not boxing it into time. Everyone who tells a story tells it differently, just to remind us that everybody sees it differently. Some people say there are true things to be found, some people say all kinds of things can be proved. I don't believe them. The only thing for certain is how complicated it all is, like string full of knots. It's all there but hard to find the beginning and impossible to fathom the end. The best you can do is admire the cat's cradle, and maybe knot it up a bit more. History should be a hammock for swinging and a game for playing, the way cats play. Claw it, chew it, rearrange it and at bedtime it's still a ball of string full of knots. Nobody should mind. Some people make a lot of money out of it. Publishers do well, children, when bright, can come top. It's an all-purpose rainy day pursuit, this reducing of stories called history.

People like to separate storytelling which is not fact from history which is fact. They do this so that they know what to believe and what not to believe. This is very curious. How is it that no one will believe that the whale swallowed Jonah when every day Jonah is swallowing the whale? I can see them now, stuffing down the fishiest of fish tales, and why? Because it is history. Knowing what to believe had its advantages. It built an empire and kept people where they belonged, in the bright realm of the wallet . . .

Very often history is a means of denying the past. Denying the past is to refuse to recognise its integrity. To fit it, force it, function it, to suck out the spirit until it looks the way you think it should. We are all historians in our small way. And in some ghastly way Pol Pot was more honest than the rest of us have been. Pol Pot decided to dispense with the past altogether. To dispense with the sham of treating the past with objective respect. In Cambodia the cities were to be wiped out, maps thrown away, everything gone. No documents. Nothing. A brave new world. The old world was horrified. We pointed the finger, but big fleas have little fleas on their back to bite them.

People have never had a problem disposing of the past when it gets too difficult. Flesh will burn, photos will burn, and memory, what is that? The imperfect ramblings of fools who will not see the need to forget. And if we can't dispose of it we can alter it. The dead don't shout. There is a certain seductiveness about what is dead. It will retain all those admirable qualities of life with none of that tiresome messiness associated with live things. Crap and complaints and the need for affection. You can auction it, museum it, collect it. It's much safer to be a collector of curios, because if you are curious, you have to sit and sit and see what happens. You have to wait on the beach until it gets cold, and you have to invest in a glass-bottomed boat, which is more expensive than a fishing rod, and puts you in the path of the elements. The curious are always in some danger. If you are curious you might never come home, like all the men who now live with mermaids at the bottom of the sea.

Or the people who found Atlantis.

When the Pilgrim Fathers set sail it was not without the opinion of many that they were crazy. History has now decided otherwise. Curious people who are explorers must bring back more than a memory or a story, they must bring home potatoes or tobacco or, best of all, gold.

But happiness is not a potato.

And El Dorado is more than Spanish gold which is why it could not exist. The ones who came home were mad with a vision that had no meaning. And so, being sensible, the collector of curios will surround himself with dead things, and think about the past when it lived and moved and had being. The collector of curios lives in a derelict railway station with a video of various trains. He is the original living dead.

So the past, because it is past, is only malleable where once it was flexible. Once it could change its mind, now it can only undergo change. The lens can be tinted, tilted, smashed. What matters is that order is seen to prevail . . . and if we are eighteenth-century gentlemen, drawing down the blinds as our coach jumbles over the Alps, we have to know what we are doing, pretending an order that doesn't exist, to make a security that cannot exist.

There is an order and a balance to be found in stories.

History is St George.

And when I look at a history book and think of the imaginative effort it has taken to squeeze this oozing world between two boards and typeset, I am astonished. Perhaps the event has an unassailable truth. God saw it. God knows. But I am not God. And so when someone tells me what they heard or saw, I believe them, and I believe their friend who also saw, but not in the same way, and I can put these accounts together and I will not have a seamless wonder but a sandwich laced with mustard of my own.

The salt beef of civilisation rumbling round in the gut. Constipation was a great problem after the Second World War. Not enough roughage in the diet, too much refined food. If you always eat out you can never be sure what's going in, and received information is nobody's exercise.

Rotten and rotting.

Here is some advice. If you want to keep your own teeth, make your own sandwiches . . .

JOSHUA

'THERE,' DECLARED MY mother, laying down the vacuum cleaner. 'You could keep a coffin in here without feeling guilty, not a speck of dust anywhere.'

Mrs White came out of the lobby waving a dish-cloth. 'I've done all them skirting boards, but me back's not what it was.'

'No,' my mother answered, shaking her head, 'these things are sent to try us.'

'Well at least we know they're holy,' said Mrs White.

The parlour was certainly very clean. I poked my head round the door and noticed that all the seat covers had been changed to our very best, my mother's wedding best, a present from her friends in France. The brasses gleamed, and Pastor Spratt's crocodile nutcracker took pride of place on the mantelpiece.

'What's all the fuss about,' I wondered. I went to check the calendar, but as far as I could see we weren't down for a house meeting, and there was no visiting preacher due on Sunday. I went into the kitchen where Mrs White was making a sad cake, a round flat pastry filled with currants and spread with butter.

For a moment she didn't notice me.

'Hello,' I said. 'What's going on?'

Mrs White turned round and gave a little screech. 'You're supposed to be at violin practice.'

'It's cancelled. Anybody else here?'

'Your mother's gone out.' She sounded a bit nervous, but then she often did.

'Well I'll take the dog out then,' I decided.

'I'm just going to the toilet,' said Mrs White, disappearing out of the back door.

'There's no paper . . .' I began, but it was too late.

We set off up the hill, climbing and climbing until the town was beaten flat. The dog ran off down a trench and I tried to spot various landmarks, like the dentist and the Rechabite Hall. I thought I might go and see Melanie that night. I had told my mother as much as I could, but not everything. I had a feeling she wouldn't really understand. Besides, I wasn't quite certain what was happening myself, it was the second time in my life that I had experienced uncertainty.

Uncertainty to me was like Aardvark to other people. A curious thing I had no notion of, but recognized through second-hand illustration. The feeling I now had in my head and stomach was the same as on that Awful Occasion, and that time, as I stood by the tea urn in the vestry, I had heard Miss Jewsbury say, 'Of course, she must feel very uncertain.' I was very upset. Uncertainty was what the Heathen felt, and I was chosen by God.

That Awful Occasion was the time my natural mother had come to claim me back. I'd had an idea that there was something curious about the circumstance of my birth, and once found my adoption papers hidden under a stack of flannels in the holiday drawer. 'Formalities,' my mother had said, waving me away. 'You were always mine, I had you from the Lord.' I didn't think about it again until there was a knock on the door one Saturday. My mother got there before me because she was praying in the parlour. I followed her down the lobby.

'Who is it Mum?'

She didn't answer.

'Who is it?'

'Go inside until I tell you.'

I slunk off, thinking it was either Jehovah's Witnesses or the man from the Labour party. Before long I could hear voices, angry voices; my mother seemed to have let the person in, which was strange. She didn't like having the Heathen in the house. 'Leaves a bad atmosphere,' she always said.

I remembered something I'd seen Mrs White do on the fornication occasion. Reaching far back into the War Cupboard, behind the dried egg, I found a wine glass and put it against the wall. It worked. I could hear every word. After five minutes I put the glass away, picked up our dog, and cried and cried and cried.

Eventually my mother came in.

'She's gone.'

'I know who she was, why didn't you tell me?'

'It's nothing to do with you.'

'She's my mother.'

No sooner had I said that than I felt a blow that wrapped round my head like a bandage. I lay on the lino looking up into the face.

'I'm your mother,' she said very quietly. 'She was a carrying case.'

'I wanted to see her.'

'She's gone and she'll never come back.' My mother turned away and locked herself in the kitchen. I couldn't think and I couldn't breathe so I started to run. I ran up the long stretchy street with the town at the bottom and the hill at the top. It was Easter time and the cross on the hill loomed big and black. 'Why didn't you tell me,' I screamed at the painted wood, and I beat the wood with my hands until my hands dropped away by themselves. When I looked out over the town, nothing had changed. Tiny figures moved up and down and the mill chimneys puffed out their usual serene smoke signals. On Ellison's Tenement they had started to run the fair. How could it be? I had rather gaze on a new ice age than these familiar things.

When I finally went home that day, my mother was watching television. She never spoke of what had happened and neither did I.

Knowing Melanie was a much happier thing, so why was I beginning to feel so uncomfortable? And why did I not always tell my mother where I stayed at night? It was usual for our church to spend time, days and nights, in each other's homes. Until Elsie got sick I stayed with her a lot, and I think she knew where I was, on the nights I didn't arrive. Melanie and I stayed there together sometimes, long sleepless nights till the light filled the window and Elsie fetched us coffee.

'Whatever do you talk about?' she scolded, as we yawned and fumbled our way through breakfast. 'Still, I was the same.'

Now that Elsie was in hospital we had to be more careful. She stayed at my house once, and my mother very carefully made up the camp bed in my room.

'We don't need it,' I told her.

'Yes you do,' she told me.

Early in the morning, about two a.m., when the World Service closed down, we heard her come slowly up the stairs to bed. I had learned to move quickly. She stood by my door for a few moments, then suddenly pushed it open. I could just see the braid at the bottom of her dressing gown. Nobody moved and then she was gone. She kept her light on all night. Soon afterwards I decided to tell her how I felt. I explained how much I wanted to be with Melanie, that I could talk to her, that I needed that kind of friend. And . . . And . . . But I never managed to talk about and . . . My mother had been very quiet, nodding her head from time to time, so that I thought she understood some of it. When I finished I gave her a little kiss, which I think surprised her a bit; we never usually touched except in anger. 'Go to bed now,' she said, picking up her Bible.

Since that time we had hardly spoken. She seemed caught up in something, and I had my own worries. Today, for the first time, she was her old self, busy, and obviously wanting company, if Mrs White was around. I wanted to know what had happened to cheer her up, so I set off down the hill again with our dog circling behind.

'Hello,' I shouted, wiping my feet on the mat. The house was quite still. She had been there recently because the coffee table in the parlour now had her Bible and Promise Box on it. She'd taken a promise out too. I looked at the rolled-up bit of paper. 'The Lord is your strength and shield.' Mrs White's coat had gone, but she'd left her dishcloth on the chair. I took it into the kitchen. There was a note on the cupboard. 'Gone to stay at Mrs White's. Come to church in the morning.'

Now my mother never stayed in other people's houses except when she went to Wigan on her business. It suited me though; I could go and stay with Melanie. So I fed our dog, had a wash and set off. As usual, when I had no money for the bus, I walked the couple of miles through the cemetery and round the back of the power station.

Melanie was doing the gardening.

'What's your mum planning tonight?' I asked her.

'She's going to the club, then staying with Auntie Irene.'

'What do you want to do?' I went on, pulling up a few weeds.

She smiled at me with those lovely cat-grey eyes and tugged at her rubber gloves.

'I'll put the kettle on for a hot water bottle.'

We talked a lot that night about our plans. Melanie really did want to be a missionary, even though it was my destiny.

'Why don't you like the idea?' she wanted to know.

'I don't like hot places, that's all, I got sunstroke in Paignton last year.'

We were quiet, and I traced the outline of her marvellous bones and the triangle of muscle in her stomach. What is it about intimacy that makes it so very disturbing?

Over breakfast the next morning she told me she intended to go to university to read theology. I didn't think it was a good thing on account of modern heresies. She thought she should understand how other people saw the world.

'But you know they're wrong,' I insisted.

'Yes, but it might be interesting, come on, we'll be late for church. You're not preaching are you?'

'No,' I said. 'I was supposed to, but they changed it.'

We bustled through the kitchen and I stood on the stairs to kiss her.

'I love you almost as much as I love the Lord,' I laughed.

She looked at me, and her eyes clouded for a moment. 'I don't know,' she said.

By the time we got to church, the first hymn was under way. My mother glared at me, and I tried to look sorry. We had slid in next to Miss Jewsbury who told me to keep calm.

'What do you mean?' I whispered.

'Come and talk to me afterwards,' she hissed, 'but not till we're out of sight.'

I decided she had gone mad. The church was very full as usual, and every time I caught someone's eye they smiled or nodded. It made me happy. There was nowhere I'd rather be. When the hymn was over I squeezed a bit closer to Melanie and tried to concentrate on the Lord. 'Still,' I thought, 'Melanie is a gift from the Lord, and it would be ungrateful not to appreciate her.' I was still deep in these contemplations when I realized that something disturbing was happening. The church had gone very quiet and the pastor was standing on his lower platform, with my mother next to him. She was weeping. I felt a searing pain against my knuckles; it was Melanie's ring. Then Miss Jewsbury was urging me to my feet saying, 'Keep calm, keep calm,' and I walking out to the front with Melanie. I shot a glance at her. She was pale.

'These children of God,' began the pastor, 'have fallen under Satan's spell.'

His hand was hot and heavy on my neck. Everyone in the congregation looked like a waxwork.

'These children of God have fallen foul of their lusts.'

'Just a minute . . . ,' I began, but he took no notice.

'These children are full of demons.'

A cry of horror ran through the church.

'I'm not,' I shouted, 'and neither is she.'

'Listen to Satan's voice,' said the pastor to the church, pointing at me. 'How are the best become the worst.'

'What are you talking about?' I asked, desperate.

'Do you deny you love this woman with a love reserved for man and wife?'

'No, yes, I mean of course I love her.'

'I will read you the words of St Paul,' announced the pastor, and he did, and many more words besides about unnatural passions and the mark of the demon.

'To the pure all things are pure,' I yelled at him. 'It's you not us.'

He turned to Melanie.

'Do you promise to give up this sin and beg the Lord to forgive you?'

'Yes.' She was trembling uncontrollably. I hardly heard what she said.

'Then go into the vestry with Mrs White and the elders will come and pray for you. It's not too late for those who truly repent.'

He turned to me.

'I love her.'

'Then you do not love the Lord.'

'Yes, I love both of them.'

'You cannot.'

'I do, I do, let me go.' But he caught my arm and held me fast.

'The church will not see you suffer, go home and wait for us to help you.'

I ran out on to the street, wild with distress. Miss Jewsbury was waiting for me.

'Come on,' she said briskly, 'let's go and get some coffee and decide what you're going to do.' I went along with her, not thinking of anything but Melanie and her loveliness.

When we reached Miss Jewsbury's house, she banged the kettle on to the gas ring, and pushed me by the fire. My teeth were chattering and I couldn't talk.

'I've known you for years and you were always headstrong, why haven't you been a bit more careful?'

I just stared into the fire.

'No one need ever have found out if you hadn't tried to explain to that mother of yours.'

'She's all right,' I murmured mechanically.

'She's mad,' replied Miss Jewsbury very certainly.

'I didn't tell her everything.'

'She's a woman of the world, even though she'd never admit it to me. She knows about feelings, especially women's feelings.'

This wasn't something I wanted to go into.

'Who told you what was going on?' I asked abruptly.

'Elsie,' she said.

'Elsie?' This was too much.

'She tried to protect you, and when she got ill that last time, she told me.'

'Why?'

'Because it's my problem too.'

At that moment I thought the demon would come and carry me off. I felt dizzy.

What on earth was she talking about? Melanie and I were special.

'Drink this.' She gave me a glass. 'It's brandy.'

'I think I'll have to lie down,' I said feebly.

I don't know how long I slept, the curtains were drawn, and my shoulders felt very heavy. At first I couldn't remember why my head hurt, then as the panic in my stomach got clearer I started to go over the morning's events.

Miss Jewsbury came in.

'Feeling better?'

'Not much,' I sighed.

'Perhaps this will help.' And she began to stroke my head and shoulders. I turned over so that she could reach my back. Her hand crept lower and lower. She bent over me; I could feel her breath on my neck. Quite suddenly I turned and kissed her. We made love and I hated it and hated it, but would not stop.

It was morning when I crept home. I had a plan to go straight off to school hoping no one would notice. I expected my mother to be in bed. I was wrong. There was a strong smell of coffee and voices coming from the parlour. As I tiptoed past, I realized they were having a prayer meeting. I got my things ready and was all packed up to leave. On the way out they caught me.

'Jeanette,' cried one of the elders, dragging me into the parlour. 'Our prayers have been answered.'

'Where did you stay last night?' asked my mother sulkily.

'I can't remember.'

'That Miss Jewsbury's I'll bet.'

'Oh, she's not holy,' piped up Mrs White.

'No,' I told them all, 'not there.'

'What does it matter?' urged the pastor. 'She's here now, and it's not too late.'

'I've got to go to school.'

'Not at all, not at all,' the pastor smiled. 'Come and sit down.'

My mother absently passed me a plate of biscuits. It was 8.30 a.m.

It was 10 p.m. that same night before the elders went home. They had spent the day praying over me, laying hands on me, urging me to repent my sins before the Lord. 'Renounce her, renounce her,' the pastor kept saying, 'it's only the demon.'

My mother made cups of tea and forgot to wash the dirty ones. The parlour was full of cups. Mrs White sat on one and cut herself, someone else spilt theirs, but they didn't stop. I still couldn't think, could only see Melanie's face and Melanie's body, and every so often the outline of Miss Jewsbury bending over me.

At 10 p.m. the pastor heaved a great sigh and offered me one last chance.

'I can't,' I said. 'I just can't.'

'We'll come back the day after tomorrow,' he confided to my mother. 'Meantime, don't let her out of this room, and don't feed her. She needs to lose her strength before it can be hers again.'

My mother nodded, nodded, nodded and locked me in. She did give me a blanket, but she took away the light bulb. Over the thirty-six hours that followed, I thought about the demon and some other things besides.

I knew that demons entered wherever there was a weak point. If I had a demon my weak point was Melanie, but she was beautiful and good and had loved me.

Can love really belong to the demon?

What sort of demon? The brown demon that rattles the ear? The red demon that dances the hornpipe? The watery demon that causes sickness? The orange demon that beguiles? Everyone has a demon like cats have fleas.

'They're looking in the wrong place,' I thought. 'If they want to get at my demon they'll have to get at me.'

I thought about William Blake.

'If I let them take away my demons, I'll have to give up what I've found.'

'You can't do that,' said a voice at my elbow.

Leaning on the coffee table was the orange demon.

'I've gone mad,' I thought.

'That may well be so,' agreed the demon evenly. 'So make the most of it.'

I flopped heavily against the settee. 'What do you want?'

'I want to help you decide what you want.' And the creature hopped up on to the mantelpiece and sat on Pastor Spratt's brass crocodile.

'Everyone has a demon as you so rightly observed,' the thing began, 'but not everyone knows this, and not everyone knows how to make use of it.'

'Demons are evil, aren't they?' I asked, worried.

'Not quite, they're just different, and difficult. You know what auras are?'

I nodded.

'Well, the demon you get depends on the colour of your aura, yours is orange which is why you've got me. Your mother's is brown, which is why she's so odd, and Mrs White's is hardly a demon at all. We're here to keep you in one piece, if you ignore us, you're quite likely to end up in two pieces, or lots of pieces, it's all part of the paradox.'

'But in the Bible you keep getting driven out.'

'Don't believe all you read.'

I started to feel ill again, so I took off my socks and pushed my toes into my mouth for comfort. They tasted of digestive biscuits. After that I went to the window and burst a few of the geranium buds to hear the pop. When I sat down the demon was glowing very bright and polishing the crocodile with its handkerchief.

'What sex are you?'

'Doesn't matter does it? After all that's your problem.'

'If I keep you, what will happen?'

'You'll have a difficult, different time.'

'Is it worth it?'

'That's up to you.'

'Will I keep Melanie?'

But the demon had vanished.

When the pastor and the elders came back, I was calm, cheerful, and ready to accept.

'I'll repent,' I said, as soon as they came in the parlour. The pastor seemed surprised.

'Are you sure?'

'Sure.' I wanted to get it over with as quickly as possible; besides, I hadn't eaten for two days. All the elders knelt down to pray, and I knelt down beside them. One of them began to speak in tongues, and it was then I felt a prickle at the back of my neck.

'Go away,' I hissed. 'They'll see you.' I opened an eye to check.

'Not them,' replied the demon, 'they talk a lot but they don't see nothing.'

'I'm not getting rid of you, this is the best way I can think of.'

'Oh, that's fine,' trilled the demon, 'I was just passing.'

By this time all the elders were singing *What a Friend We Have in Jesus* so I thought it wise to join in. It was all over very quickly really, and my mother had put a joint in the oven.

'I hope you'll testify on Sunday,' said the pastor, hugging me.

'Yes,' I said, squashed. 'What will Melanie do?'

'She's gone away for a while,' Mrs White put in. 'To recover. You'll see how much better she is in a few weeks.'

'Where's she gone?' I demanded.

'Don't you worry,' the pastor soothed. 'She'll be safe with the Lord.'

As soon as they had all left I went straight round to Miss Jewsbury's.

'Do you know where she is?'

She opened the door wide. 'I'll tell you in a little while.'

Melanie was staying with relatives in Halifax. I told my mother I had to spend the night in the church. She seemed to understand, and so I made Miss Jewsbury drive me the twenty-five miles across to where I needed to be.

'You'll pick me up at 7 a.m.?'

She nodded, biting her lip.

'You know I have to see her, make sure I'm safe.'

As soon as it grew shadowy I rang the door bell.

'Is Melanie here?' I asked the woman. 'I'm her friend from school.'

'Yes, come in.'

'No, I won't thanks, I'll just give her a message, if she'll come out.' Melanie came to the door. When she saw me she tried to shut it.

'I've got to talk to you,' I begged. 'Go upstairs in about half an hour, I'll go up now and wait for you.' She nodded, and let me slip past. I heard her say goodbye very loudly and shut the door. No one seemed to think anything of it.

It was a crisis and once again I fell asleep.

In front of me was a great stone arena, crumbling in places, but still visibly round. At the far end, truck-loads of men and women were being emptied out on to the grass; most were mutilated, all had numbers round their necks, and I heard a guard say, 'This is your new address.' The prisoners were very quiet and marched without resistance towards a massive stone turret. In the turret were little nooks with numbers that corresponded to the numbers around the pris-oners' necks. In the middle of the turret an iron stairway spiralled up and up; I started to climb, along with many others, but each time we passed one of the nooks, its inmate tried to push us off. I was the only person left when the stairway stopped in front of a glass door. The letters on the door spelt BOOK-SHOP: OPEN. I went inside, there was a woman at the counter, a number of buyers and browsers, and a team of young women translating *Beowulf*.

'Hello,' called the assistant. 'Why don't you start as a browser and take over from one of the girls when it's time to move round?'

'Where am I?'

'Where everyone is who can't make the ultimate decision, this is the city of Lost Chances, and this, the Room of the Final Disappointment. You see, you can climb as high as you like, but if you've already made the Fundamental Mistake, you end up here, in this room. You can change your role, but never your circumstance. It's too late for all that now, toodle-ooo, I'm about to become a buyer.'

'Jeanette,' said Melanie, 'I think you've got a temperature.'

She was sitting beside me, drinking a cup of tea. She looked tired and crumpled like a balloon full of old air. I touched her cheek but she winced and pulled away.

'What did they do to you?' I asked.

'Nothing, I repented, and they told me I should try and go away for a week. We can't see each other, it's wrong.' She started to tug at the quilt and I couldn't bear it anymore. I think we cried each other to sleep, but somewhere in the night I stretched out to her and kissed her and kissed her until we were both sweating and crying with mixed up bodies and swollen faces. She was still asleep when I heard Miss Jewsbury sound her horn.

The next thing that happened to me was glandular fever.

'It's her Humours,' my mother pronounced.

Certainly it was the belief of the Faithful that God

was cleansing me of all my demons, and there was no doubt that I would be welcomed back into the fold as soon as I recovered.

'The Lord forgives and forgets,' the pastor told me.

Perhaps the Lord does, but my mother didn't. While I lay shivering in the parlour she took a toothcomb to my room and found all the letters, all the cards, all the jottings of my own, and burnt them one night in the backyard. There are different sorts of treachery, but betrayal is betrayal wherever you find it. She burnt a lot more than the letters that night in the backyard. I don't think she knew. In her head she was still queen, but not my queen any more, not the White Queen any more. Walls protect and walls limit. It is in the nature of walls that they should fall. That walls should fall is the consequence of blowing your own trumpet.

The Forbidden City lies ransacked now and the topless towers are all gone. Only a stone's throw separates the Black Prince from Amiens, and a pebble will fell a warrior today. Old men that dribble and huddle on any of these benches will tell you where their sweetheart's house once stood, will tell you how her garden grew, and how they daily beat a path to her door.

She had a heart of stone.

Who will cast the first stone?

Where the world ends in the East you will find a stone lion, and in the West, a gryphon made of stone. At the Northern corner a stone turret will baffle you, and in the South a gritty beach for your feet. Do not be afraid. These are the ancients. Weathered and wise as they are, respect them, but they are not the everlasting substance. The body that contains a spirit is the one true god.

It is the nature of stone to convert bone.

At one time or another there will be a choice: you or the wall.

Humpty Dumpty sat on the wall.

Humpty Dumpty had a great fall.

The City of Lost Chances is full of those who chose the wall.

All the king's horses and all the king's men.

Couldn't put Humpty together again.

Then is it necessary to wander unprotected through the land?

It is necessary to distinguish the chalk circle from the stone wall.

Is it necessary to live without a home?

It is necessary to distinguish physics from metaphysics.

Yet many of the principles are the same.

They are, but in the cities of the interior all things are changed.

A wall for the body, a circle for the soul.

'Here you are,' said my mother, giving me a sharp dig in the side. 'Some fruit. You're rambling in your sleep again.'

It was a bowl of oranges.

I took out the largest and tried to peel it. The skin hung stubborn, and soon I lay panting, angry and defeated. What about grapes or bananas? I did finally pull away the outer shell and, cupping both hands round, tore open the fruit.

'Feeling any better?' Sitting in the middle was the orange demon.

'I'm going to die.'

'Not you, in fact you're recovering, apart from a few minor hallucinations, and remember, you've made your choice now, there's no going back.'

'What are you talking about? I haven't made any choice.' I was struggling to sit up.

'Catch,' called the demon and vanished. In my hand was a rough brown pebble.

By that summer I was my old self again. Melanie had gone away before starting university, and I was preparing my sermons for a tent mission we had all planned in Blackpool. No one mentioned the Incident, and no one seemed to notice that Miss Jewsbury had picked up her oboe and left. My mother spent most of her time singing *Bringing in the Sheaves*, and collecting tins for the Harvest Festival. She disapproved of perishables on account of the Holocaust, and had made it her campaign to persuade the other church women to contribute to a giant War Cupboard hidden beneath the vestry. 'They'll thank me when the time comes,' she always said.

So one sunny Saturday we piled into the bus and set off for Blackpool.

'I wish we had Elsie with that accordion,' Mrs Rothwell sighed.

'She's better where she is,' returned my mother rather sharply.

In the past these remarks would have meant nothing to me, now I wasn't so easy. I had often thought of questioning her, trying to make her tell me how she saw the world. I used to imagine we saw things just the same, but all the time we were on different planets.

I went to sit at the back to help May with her pools. My mother obviously felt slighted at my departure and buried herself in the *Band of Hope* review.

'It's a funny bugger that one,' said May sourly.

By now I was inclined to agree.

Our first meeting that night was a great success. I was down to preach, and as usual a great number found the Lord.

'She's lost none of her gifts, has she?' May grinned at my mother.

'I got to her in time, that's why,' was all my mother could say, and she went back to the guest house. After she and a few others had left, the rest of us decided to rejoice in the Lord. We got out the tambourines and the chorus sheets, and praised far into the night. At about 11 p.m. the tent flap billowed, and we heard a great commotion in the field outside.

'It's the Holy Spirit,' cried May.

'It doesn't sound holy to me,' declared Mrs White.

'What shall we do?' whispered one of the newly converted to me. I put my arm round her. She was very soft. 'I'll go and see,' I reassured everyone.

'If it's the Lord, don't look,' May urged as I disappeared through the flap.

It wasn't the Lord, it was five angry men from the boarding house nearby. They had lanterns and a few bits of paper that they waved at me.

'Are you in charge?'

'Yes, you could say that. I'm leading the prayer meeting, come in.' They followed me into the tent.

'We don't care about no prayer meeting . . . ,' one of them began.

'The Lord strike you down,' spat Mrs Rothwell, who had just woken up.

'What we do care about,' he continued, glaring at us, 'is a decent night's sleep for decent folks. We're here on our holidays, and we don't want no holy Joes banging 'n' screaming fit to wake dead.'

'On the last day the dead will walk, and you'll be with goats,' May said scornfully.

'Listen you.' One of the others came forward poking his paper at her. 'It says here, in these boarding house regulations, that there's no din after eleven o'clock. This is boarding house field you're all on.'

'Come and join us,' I suggested.

'Look, we work all year round at the British Rope Factory in bloody Wakefield, and we come here for a bit of peace, so stop it or cop it.' There was a moment's silence, then,

'Come on lads, let's git to bloody bed.'

'Well,' breathed Mrs White.

'No point,' I said. 'We can start again tomorrow, let's pack up.' And so the Faithful put away their joyful noises, leaving me and newly converted Katy to blow out the lanterns.

When I got back to the guest house my mother and I had taken, she was lying propped up against the pillows reading her new book from Pastor Spratt. This one was called *Where White Man Fears to Tread*.

'Do you know,' she said, 'they fed these white mice on the same food as Injuns eat and they all died.'

'So?'

'So it just shows the Lord provides for Christian countries.'

'I don't think they'd survive any better on hot pot.'

'Beezum, thank the Lord for his goodness, now I want to go to sleep,' and she put out her little light, and began to snore.

As for me, I had other things to think about.

The following day we were all due to meet under the tower to give out tracts for the coming evening's meeting. May had her big sandwich board that said SEEK YE THE LORD WHILE HE MAY BE FOUND. 'My name's in that text,' she told everyone, with pride, 'so I know it's me duty to carry it.' We did quite well, for a tract session, we had three street conversions, and a few people who promised to come back for the night. 'Afternoon off,' the pastor told everyone.

'What about the zoo?' asked May perkily. 'I want to see them little monkeys.'

'She's coming up the tower with me,' announced my mother stiffly, 'they've got an exhibition of great film stars.'

'I'm going for a walk on the prom,' I told them both, and set off.

Katy sat in a deckchair and Katy looked at the sun.

Katy ate an ice-cream and Katy looked like fun.

'Hello.' I sat down beside her. 'Are you staying near here?'

'No, I came on the tram, thought I might as well in time for tonight.'

'You don't live far away from our church at home though do you?'

'No, Oswaldtwistle is where we live, it's a bus ride.'

'Well, we'll see each other then.'

She looked at me for a moment, and I thought it best to go and inspect the gospel tent . . .

It had been a glorious week. Many of the souls who found the Lord lived close by our main church, and those who came from far away were given letters of introduction to their closest meeting house. On the last day of our campaign we held an open air thanksgiving on the beach, which would have ended everything perfectly, had not Mrs Rothwell gone off by herself to commune with the Spirit. She was old and deaf and so engrossed that she never saw the tide come sloping in.

'Are we all here?' The pastor counted as we filed on to the bus. 'Who's got the banner?'

'Me,' shouted May from over the wheel arch.

'That it then?' asked Fred, our hired driver.

'Except for Mrs Rothwell.' Alice pointed to the empty seat.

We looked about us, and only by a miracle were we in time to catch sight of Mrs Rothwell's waving arm as she sank below the surf.

'Is she waving?' May wondered anxiously.

'Drowning more like,' exclaimed Fred, peeling off his jacket and tie. 'Don't fret, I won all the badges in me youth.' And he thundered off through the breakers. Immediately the pastor led everyone in prayer, and Mrs White started up with *We Have an Anchor*. We had hardly got to verse 3 when Fred reappeared carrying Mrs Rothwell over his shoulder.

'Fred, her underslip's showing,' tutted my mother, tugging as best she could.

'Niver mind her underslip, what about my blue suede shoes?'

They were ruined.

'Is she still with us?' the pastor interrupted impatiently.

'Oh I am, I am,' wailed Mrs Rothwell from some-where in the middle of Fred's spine. 'I thought I would be in glory this time.'

'But you were signalling for help.'

'Nay, I were waving goodbye.'

'I said she were waving.'

'Someone give her a towel,' the pastor shooed, 'and let this poor man drive us home.'

Fred squelched to the cab muttering about compensation and why he bloody bothered and with a sudden flood of exhaust we were off.

The Harvest Festival came and went, my mother having achieved a record number of tins for the War Cupboard, with plenty left over to distribute to the poor. Not everyone was satisfied.

'What do I want with four tins of black cherries and them water chestnuts in brine?' blind Nellie grumbled when my father took her carrier bag. 'In the old days, we got bread and fruit and a few nice bits of veg. It's new-fangledness, that's what it is.'

When my mother heard about this, she was furious, and crossed Nellie off her prayer list. My dad put her on his instead, so she didn't miss out. Then as the wind got up and the nights started drawing in we turned our thoughts to Nativity, and how best to explain the Christmas message. As usual we were going to take a stake in the town hall crib, and gather under the Heathen pine to sing Christmas carols. This meant regular rehearsals with the Salvation Army, always a problem because our tambourine players invariably lost the beat. This year, the General wondered if we'd like to stick to singing.

'It sez make a joyful noise,' May reminded him.

When the General ventured to suggest a less than literal interpretation of this psalm, there was uproar. For a start it was heresy. Then it was rude. Then it meant dissension amongst our flock. Some of us could see the sense of it, some of us were outraged. We argued until the tea and biscuits came round, then the General made his own decision. Anyone who wanted to play the tambourine might do so in their own church, not in his rehearsals, and not at the carol singing itself.

'I'll be off then,' said May.

We looked at one another.

'We'll all be off,' I told the General. 'Thanks for the tea.'

In the porch of the Quaker Assembly Rooms we found May crying.

'Eh luv, don't.' Someone put their arm round her. 'It's nowt.'

'After all me work,' sobbed May.

'It's only Sally Army, you don't need them.'

'Let's go round to my house,' suggested Mrs White, 'and make a plan.'

That night at Mrs White's we were sure the Lord was guiding us, the Sisterhood Choir and the Male Voice Choir would join forces and we'd take our space at the town hall and even go out to the high-ways and byways. We had four tambourine players, all taught by May, my guitar and mandolin, and possibly my mother's harmonium, if it didn't get too cold.

'We don't need them trumpets anyway.'

The next problem was who should write the script for the Nativity play. It was unanimously decided it ought to be mother, on account of her education.

'Such a one for figures as you never saw,' May said admiringly.

My mother blushed and said she couldn't and accepted. She bought typing paper and a new dictionary and told my dad and me to do as best we could. She had the Lord's work to do. All through the following day she scribbled and sighed in the parlour, surrounded by cheese sandwiches and pictures of Bethlehem in winter. At four o'clock she pushed a fat envelope into my hands and told me to send it airmail.

'It's the last posting day for Pastor Spratt.' Then she was gone.

I was too busy teaching my Bible study class on doctrine to pay much attention to my mother. Katy had been coming to church ever since her conversion in the summer, and had proved a lively addition. She was a particular help to me, often typing out my sermons when they had to go in the district newsletter. I hadn't seen the orange demon for ages, so I felt that my life must be back to normal.

Soon came the Sunday of the Nativity play. The children had rehearsed for weeks, and my father had built the set. My mother wore a new hat and I sat next to Katy, holding the prompt boards. The church was full of the Heathen come to see their offspring perform. Even Mrs Arkwright from the vermin shop was there. 'Little Donkey' went well, and the first scene, 'No Room at the Inn', was under way, when the side door opened and a figure slipped in trying to be quiet. I squinted through the darkness; it looked familiar.

'Oh Joseph, we'll have to sleep in the stable.'

There was just something about the way it sat . . .

'Don't worry Mary, others have it hard too' (there was great emphasis on the 'h').

The halo of hair was getting more visible as the shepherds scuttled on with their lanterns.

The last I heard that evening was 'Do not fear, I bring you tidings of great joy.' At the back of the church was Melanie.

As soon as the service ended I left my mother to her triumph and went home. I was trembling with fear. As far as I was concerned Melanie was dead. No one mentioned her, and as her mother never came to church, there was no need to remember. At nine o'clock there was a knock on the door. I knew who it was, but praying it might be carol singers I went to answer it, in faith, with a few ready pennies.

'Hello,' she said. 'Can I come in?'

I moved to let her pass. She had put on some weight and looked quite serene. Over the half hour that followed she chatted about her course, her friends, her holiday plans. Did I want to go for a walk with her one day?

No.

She said her mother intended to move away soon, far away, down south. This would be Melanie's last time behind the power station. I should come and say goodbye to her mother.

No.

At last she put on her gloves and beret and very lightly kissed me goodbye. I felt nothing. But when she'd gone, I pulled up my knees under my chin, and begged the Lord to set me free.

Thankfully, it was a busy time. The day after we were all due down at the town hall to sing our carols, the Sally Army permitting. We had a grand time at first. May had bought new ribbons for her tambourine, and my mother was playing the harmonium under a huge green fishing umbrella lent by the Christian Anglers' Association.

'What about *The Holly and the Ivy*?'

'Too pagan.'

'What about *We Three Kings*?'

'You start then.'

And we did. We drew a big crowd that day. Some came to laugh, but most put a contribution in the tin and joined in on the ones they knew. I saw Melanie standing with a bunch of mistletoe. She waved across the heads, but I pretended not to see. Then the Salvation Army arrived and began to put up their music stands. They'd brought the drum. People watched and waited, and sure enough, within ten minutes there were two sets of carols going strong. My mother pumped and puffed as best she could, and May banged so hard that she split the skin. All the people who had been standing by the barrel organ at the side of the fish market came running round to find out what was happening. Then someone took a photograph.

'It's that bloody drum,' wheezed May. 'We'll not win.' There was some mumbling on our side, then we all agreed to go to Trickett's to get warm. As we trooped in we saw Mrs Clifton sitting by herself with a teapot.

'Mind if I sit down?' panted May, forcing herself on to one of the stools.

'I was leaving anyway,' announced Mrs Clifton, gathering up her Marks and Spencers carrier bags. 'Come along Toto.' And she and her Pekinese trotted off.

'Stuck-up thing,' sniffed May. 'Oy, Betty, come and give us Horlicks and a bit of sticky tape to mend this bloody job.' She waved her severed tambourine.

'I were having a quiet afternoon,' said Betty indignantly as we filled the tiny cafe. 'It's tea for all of you and I'm not doing any meals.'

Once my mother arrived with the umbrella and the harmonium I thought it best to leave. On the way to the bus stop I felt a hand on my shoulder and there was Melanie, still serene and smiling, ready to catch the same bus as me.

'Want an orange?' she offered as we sat close, in a steady silence. She made to peel it. I grabbed her arm.

'No, don't do that. I mean I'll be having tea soon. Don't waste it.'

Again she smiled and talked of this and that, until at last it was my stop and hers, miles away. I jumped up, jumped off and ran as fast as I could, while Melanie gazed benignly from the top deck.

I had to head the Bible study that night, despite my sudden nervousness and the worry that I was getting ill again. Katy was there, and saw my troubled face, and wanted to help. 'Come and stay this weekend,' she offered, 'we'll have to sleep in the caravan, but it won't be cold.' I hadn't stayed anywhere for a long time. I thought it might do me good.

On the banks of the Euphrates find a secret garden cunningly walled. There is an entrance, but the entrance is guarded. There is no way in for you. Inside you will find every plant that grows growing circular-wise like a target. Close to the heart is a sundial and at the heart an orange tree. This fruit had tripped up athletes while others have healed their wounds. All true quests end in this garden, where the split fruit pours forth blood and the halved fruit is a full bowl for travellers and pilgrims. To eat of the fruit means to leave the garden because the fruit speaks of other things, other longings. So at dusk you say goodbye to the place you love, not knowing if you can ever return, knowing you can never return by the same way as this. It may be, some other day, that you will open a gate by chance, and find yourself again on the other side of the wall.

'I'll bring in the calor gas,' said Katy, 'so we won't be cold.'

We weren't cold, not that night nor any of the others we spent together over the years that followed. She was my most uncomplicated love affair, and I loved her because of it. She seemed to have no worries at all, and though she still denies it, I think she planned the caravan.

'Are you sure this is what you want?' I murmured, not intending to stop.

'Oh yes,' she cried, 'yes.'

We stopped talking about it quickly because the dialogue was getting too embarrassing. She was blissful. I took care never to look at her when I preached, though she always sat in the front row. We did have a genuinely spiritual dimension. I taught her a lot, and she put all her efforts into the church, quite apart from me. It was a good time. To the pure all things are pure . . .

A year had passed since Melanie's Easter and my illness. It was Easter time again and the Church of

England was winding its way up the hill, carrying the cross. On Palm Sunday Melanie returned, beaming with an important announcement. She was to be married that autumn to an army man. To be fair he had given up the bad fight for the Good Fight, but as far as I was concerned he was revolting. I had no quarrel with men. At that time there was no reason that I should. The women in our church were strong and organized. If you want to talk in terms of power I had enough to keep Mussolini happy. So I didn't object to Melanie getting married, I objected to her getting married to *him*. And she was serene, serene to the point of being bovine. I was so angry I tried to talk to her about it, but she had left her brain in Bangor. She asked me what I was doing.

'Doing for what?'

She blushed. I had no intention of telling her or anyone else what happened between Katy and me. Not by nature discreet or guilty I had enough memory to know where that particular revelation would lead. She left the day after, to stay with *him* and his parents. Just as they were driving off on his horrible Iron Curtain motor bike, he patted my arm, told me he knew, and forgave us both. There was only one thing I could do; mustering all my spit, I did it.

JUDGES

'Now I give you fair warning' shouted the Queen, stamping
on the ground as she spoke; *'Either you or your head must
be off.'*

MY MOTHER WANTED me to move out, and she
had the backing of the pastor and most of the
congregation, or so she said. I made her ill, made the
house ill, brought evil into the church. There was no
escaping this time. I was in trouble. Picking up my
Bible, the hill seemed the only place to go just then.
On the top of the hill is a stone mound to hide
behind when the wind blows. The dog never worked
it out; used it to pee against, or to play hide and seek
with me, but still stood ears flattened and water-eyed
till I slung her up in my jacket, warming both of us.
The dog was a tiny and foolhardy Lancashire heeler,
brown and black with pointy ears. She slept in an
Alsatians' basket which might have been her problem.
She didn't show that she knew what size she really
was, she fought with every other dog we met, and
snapped at passers by. Once, trying to reach a huge
icicle, I fell down on to a quarry ledge and couldn't
climb back again; the earth kept crumbling away. She
barked and spluttered and then ran off to help me.
Now, here we were, on a different edge.

It all seemed to hinge around the fact that I loved

the wrong sort of people. Right sort of people in every respect except this one; romantic love for another woman was a sin.

'Aping men,' my mother had said with disgust.

Now if I was aping men she'd have every reason to be disgusted. As far as I was concerned men were something you had around the place, not particularly interesting, but quite harmless. I had never shown the slightest feeling for them, and apart from my never wearing a skirt, saw nothing else in common between us. Then I remembered the famous incident of the man who'd come to our church with his boyfriend. At least, they were holding hands. 'Should have been a woman that one,' my mother had remarked.

This was clearly not true. At that point I had no notion of sexual politics, but I knew that a homosexual is further away from a woman than a rhinoceros. Now that I do have a number of notions about sexual politics, this early observation holds good. There are shades of meaning, but a man is a man, wherever you find it. My mother has always given me problems because she is enlightened and reactionary at the same time. She didn't believe in Determinism and Neglect, she believed that you made people and yourself what you wanted. Anyone could be saved and anyone could fall to the Devil, it was their choice. While some of our church forgave me on the admittedly dubious grounds that I couldn't help it (they had read Havelock Ellis and knew about Inversion), my mother saw it as a wilful act on my part to sell my soul. At first, for me, it had been an accident. That accident had forced me to think more carefully about my own instincts and others' attitudes. After the exorcism I had tried to replace my world with another just like it, but I couldn't. I loved God and I loved the church, but I began to see that as more and more complicated. It didn't help that I had no intention of becoming a missionary.

'But that's what your training's for,' my mother had wailed.

'I can preach just as well at home.'

'Oh, you'll get married and get involved.' She was bitter.

Odd that I was obviously not going to get married. I thought at first she would have been pleased. A complicated mind, my mother had.

Sir Perceval, the youngest of Arthur's knights, at last set forth from Camelot. The king had begged him not to go; he knew this was no ordinary quest. Since the visit of the Holy Grail one feast day, the mood had changed. They were brothers, they laughed at Sir Gawain and his exploits in the land of the green knight, they were brave, all brave, and their loyalty was to the king . . . Had been to the king. The Round Table and the high-walled castle were almost symbols now. Once they were meat and drink. But for Launcelot and Bors, betrayal is in the future as well as in the past. Launcelot is gone, driven mad by heavy things. Somewhere he is searching too; reports reach the king; garbled, incoherent, ragged like the men who bring them. The hall is empty. Soon the enemy will come. There was a stone that held a bright sword and no one could pull the sword because their minds were fixed on the stone.

Arthur sits on the wide steps. The Round Table is

decorated with every plant that grows growing circular-wise like a target. Near the centre is a sundial and at the centre a thorny crown. Dusty now, but all things turn to dust.

Arthur thinks of before, when there were lights and smiles.

There was a woman, he remembers her. But oh, Sir Perceval, come and turn cartwheels again.

Katy and I had gone away together for a week at the Morecambe guest house for the bereaved. It was the slack season, so anyone could go, grieving or not, though they were always very strict in winter. Katy's family were on holiday in their caravan nearby, so we were considered safe. I had been careful to keep any letters in my Saturday job locker, and as far as I could tell, we were above suspicion. We were careless though, that first night on holiday. The thought of having a whole week alone left us over-eager and I forgot to lock the door. She had pulled me on to the bed, then I noticed a thin shaft of light staining the carpet by the edge of the bed. My neck prickled and my mouth went dry. Someone was standing at the door. We didn't move, and after a moment the light disappeared. Flopping down by Katy's side I squeezed her hand tight, and promised her we'd think of something.

We did. The plan was the most fanciful of my brilliant career and from her point of view it worked perfectly. There was no hope for me.

At breakfast time we were summoned to the office of my mother's old friend and erstwhile treasurer of the Society for the Lost.

'I want the truth,' she said, not looking at either of us, 'and don't think you fool me.'

I told her that my affair with Melanie had never really ended. That Melanie had written to me for months and that finally, torn with love myself, I had begged Katy to help me arrange a meeting.

'This was the one place I thought we would be safe,' I told her as I wept.

She believed me. She wanted to. I knew she wouldn't fancy explaining to Katy's family, and I knew she wanted to upset my mother as much as possible. Forcing all the blame on me would do that. She told me to pack and be ready to leave by the morning. She wanted her letter to arrive home before I did. Katy was safe, that was the important thing. She was stubborn and angry like me, but unlike me she couldn't cope with the darker side of our church. I'd seen her kick against it before, seen her kick and cry. I was determined that they shouldn't start the demon stuff on her. I was supposed to spend the rest of the day in prayer, Melanie presumably gone. I spent it in bed with Katy. 'What will you do?' she asked, her arm tucked into mine as we walked the beach early the following day.

The sand was full of sprats gasping as the tide left them behind. As I left Katy behind, she was crying. I didn't know what to expect, but I knew I wouldn't live through any of that again. Hands in my pockets, I played with a rough brown pebble.

Of course the scene at home had been incredible. My mother smashed every plate in the kitchenette.

'There's no supper,' she told her husband when he

came in off the late shift. 'There's nothing to eat it off.' He went to the fish and chip shop and ate them at the counter.

'Oh I'm a fool to meself,' she thundered. 'Keeping you as long as I have, letting you do more exams, and for what?' She shook me. 'For what?' I pulled away.

'Leave me alone.'

'You'll be left alone soon enough.' And she went round to the telephone box to call the pastor.

When she came back, she ordered me to bed, and it seemed best to obey. My bed was narrow. I lay in it, unable to forgive myself, unable to forgive her. At regular intervals I heard her calling on the Lord to send a sign. Certainly the pastor arrived, but glad as she was, I think she would have preferred something a bit more spectacular, like for me and my bedroom to be consumed with flames while the rest of the house escaped. Downstairs, they talked in low voices for a long time. I was almost asleep when the pastor appeared with my mother hovering in the background. He stood a safe distance away like I was infected. I put my head under the pillow because I couldn't think of anything else to do. The pastor snatched it away and explained to me as quietly as he could that I was the victim of a great evil. That I was afflicted and oppressed, that I had deceived the flock. 'The demon,' he announced very slowly, 'had returned sevenfold.'

My mother gave a little cry, and then got angry again. It was my own fault. My own perversity. They started arguing between themselves about whether I was an unfortunate victim or a wicked person. I listened for a while; neither of them were very convincing, and besides, seven ripe oranges had just dropped on to the window sill.

'Have an orange,' I offered, by way of conversation. They both stared at me like I was mad. 'They're over there.' I pointed to the window.

'She's raving,' said my mother, incredulous. (She hated mad people.)

'It's her master speaking,' replied the pastor gravely. 'Ignore her, I shall take this case to the council, it's too hard for me. Keep an eye on her, but let her go to church.'

My mother nodded, sobbing and biting her lip. They left me in peace. I lay for a long time just watching the oranges. They were pretty, but not much help. I was going to need more than an icon to get me through this one.

The day after, I did go to the Sisterhood meeting. It was the first time Elsie had been at church since her long spell in hospital. She knew what was happening, but still held me close and told me not to be silly. 'Come for a cup after this,' she decided, 'but don't tell t'others.'

The meeting was near-hysterical with the strain of them all wondering what to do. Mrs White kept banging the wrong notes, and Alice lost the thread of her message when she caught me looking at her. We were thankful when nine o'clock came and it was over. No one asked me why I was leaving before the tea came round, they must have assumed Elsie was tired or I'm sure they'd have tried to stop her. When I got back to Elsie's it was the first time anyone had talked to me about Miss Jewsbury.

'She's living in Leeds,' Elsie told me, 'teaching music in one of them special schools. She's not living alone.' She gazed at me shrewdly. 'It were me that told her about you.'

I was astonished. I didn't really believe Elsie had known. She said she'd just been able to see it.

'If I'd bin around none of that trouble would have happened anyway. I would have sorted both of you out, but with being in and out of that damn hospital . . .'

I got up and hugged her and we sat by the fire together like we used to, not saying much. We didn't talk about *it*, not the rights or wrongs or anything; she looked after me by giving me what I most needed, an ordinary time with a friend.

'I have to go now Elsie.' I got up, sadly, as the clock ticked on.

'Well come back as you need.'

She stood at the door till I was a long way down the street, then as I turned to wave again, she disappeared inside. I plodded on past the viaduct and the carpet shop, then the short cut down the Factory Bottoms. I met Mrs Arkwright staggering out of the pub, The Cock and Whistle, where nobody good ever went. She beamed at me, ''Ello nipper,' and rolled on her way. Past the school house and the Methodist Chapel, and Black Abbey Street where someone had had their head chopped off. For a moment I leaned on the wall; the stone was warm, and through the window I could see a family round the fire. Their tea table had been left, chairs, table and the right number of cups. I watched the fire flicker behind the glass, then one of them got up to close the curtains.

I lingered outside my own front door for a few minutes before going in. I still didn't know what to do, wasn't even sure what the choices were or what the conflicts were; it was clear to the others, but not clear to me, and nobody seemed likely to explain. My mother was waiting for me. I was late, but I didn't tell her about Elsie, I didn't trust her to understand.

The days lingered on in a kind of numbness, me in ecclesiastical quarantine, them in a state of fear and anticipation. By Sunday the pastor had word back from the council. The real problem, it seemed, was going against the teachings of St Paul, and allowing women power in the church. Our branch of the church had never thought about it, we'd always had strong women, and the women organized everything. Some of us could preach, and quite plainly, in my case, the church was full because of it. There was uproar, then a curious thing happened. My mother stood up and said she believed this was right: that women had specific circumstances for their ministry, that the Sunday School was one of them, the Sisterhood another, but the message belonged to the men. Until this moment my life had still made some kind of sense. Now it was making no sense at all. My mother droned on about the importance of missionary work for a woman, that I was clearly such a woman, but had spurned my call in order to wield power on the home front, where it was inappropriate. She ended by saying that having taken on a man's world in other ways I had flouted God's law and tried to do it sexually. This was no spontaneous speech. She and the pastor had talked about it already. It was her weakness for the ministry that had done it. No doubt she'd told Pastor Spratt months ago. I looked around me. Good people, simple people, what would happen to them now? I knew my mother hoped I would blame myself, but I didn't. I knew now where the blame lay. If there's such a thing as spiritual adultery, my mother was a whore.

So there I was, my success in the pulpit being the reason for my downfall. The devil had attacked me at my weakest point: my inability to realize the limitations of my sex.

A voice from the back. 'That's a load of old twaddle and you know it. Now are we helping this child or not?' It was Elsie. Someone tried to sit her down, but she kept struggling and then she started coughing and then she fell over.

'Elsie.' I ran down to the back, but got pulled away.

'She can do without you.' The others gathered round while I stood helpless and shaking.

'Get a warm coat and let's get her home.' And they bundled her out into the porch.

While this was going on the pastor came up to me and said that as a mark of new obedience to the Lord I was to give up all preaching, Bible study classes and any form of what he called 'influential contact'. As soon as I had agreed he would arrange for a further more powerful exorcism and then I was to go on holiday with my mother for a fortnight to the Morecambe guest house.

'I'll tell you in the morning,' I promised, pleading tiredness.

Sir Perceval has been in the wood for many days now. His armour is dull, his horse tired. The last food he ate was a bowl of bread and milk given to him by an old woman. Other knights have been this way, he can see their tracks, their despair, for one, even his bones. He has heard tell of a ruined chapel, or an old church, no one is sure, only sure that it lies disused and holy, far away from prying eyes. Perhaps there he will find it. Last night Sir Perceval dreamed of the Holy Grail borne on a shaft of sunlight moving towards him. He reached out crying but his hands were full of thorns and he was awake. Tonight, bitten and bruised, he dreams of Arthur's court, where he was the darling, the favourite. He dreams of his hounds and his falcon, his stable and his faithful friends. His friends are dead now. Dead or dying. He dreams of Arthur sitting on a wide stone step, holding his head in his hands. Sir Perceval falls to his knees to clasp his lord, but his lord is a tree covered in ivy. He wakes, his face bright with tears.

When the pastor came round the next morning, I felt better. We had a cup of tea, the three of us; I think my mother told a joke. It was settled.

'Shall I book you in for the holiday then?' the pastor asked, fiddling for his diary. 'She's expecting you, but it's only polite.'

'How's Elsie?' This was bothering me.

The pastor frowned and said that last night had upset her more than they had realized. She had gone back into hospital for a check-up.

'Will she be all right?'

My mother pointed out that was for the Lord to decide, and we had other things to think about. The pastor smiled gently, and asked again when we wanted to go.

'I'm not going.'

He told me I'd need a rest after the struggle. That my mother needed a rest.

'She can go. I'm leaving the church, so you can forget the rest.'

They were dumbfounded. I held on tight to the little brown pebble and hoped they'd go away. They didn't. They reasoned and pleaded and stormed and took a break and came back. They even offered me my Bible class, though under supervision. Finally the pastor shook his head and declared me one of the people in Hebrews, to whom it is impossible to speak the truth. He asked me one last time:

'Will you repent?'

'No.' And I stared at him till he looked away. He took my mother off into the parlour for half an hour. I don't know what they did in there, but it didn't matter; my mother had painted the white roses red and now she claimed they grew that way.

'You'll have to leave,' she said. 'I'm not havin' demons here.'

Where could I go? Not to Elsie's, she was too sick, and no one in the church would really take the risk. If I went to Katy's there would be problems for her, and all my relatives, like most relatives, were revolting.

'I don't have anywhere to go,' I argued, following her into the kitchen.

'The Devil looks after his own,' she threw back, pushing me out.

I knew I couldn't cope, so I didn't try. I would let the feeling out later, when it was safe. For now, I had to be hard and white. In the frosty days, in the winter, the ground is white, then the sun rises, and the frosts melt . . .

'It's decided then.' I breezed in to my mother with more bravado than courage, 'I'm moving out on Thursday.'

'Where to?' She was suspicious.

'I'm not telling you, I'll see how it goes.'

'You've got no money.'

'I'll work evenings as well as weekends.'

In fact I was scared to death and going to live with a teacher who had some care for what was happening. I was driving an ice-cream van on Saturdays; now I would work Sundays as well, and try to pay the woman as best I could. Bleak, but not so bleak as staying there. I wanted the dog, but knew she wouldn't let me, so I took my books and my instruments in a tea chest, with my Bible on top. The only thing that worried me was the thought of having to work on a fruit stall. Spanish Navels, Juicy Jaffas, Ripe Sevilles.

'I won't,' I consoled myself. 'I'll go in the tripe works first.'

I made my bed carefully the last morning at home, emptied the waste paper basket, and trailed the dog on a long walk. She ran off with the Jack from the bowling green. At that time I could not imagine what would become of me, and I didn't care. It was not judgement day, but another morning.

RUTH

A LONG TIME AGO, when the kingdom was divided up into separate compartments like a pressure cooker, people took travelling a lot more seriously than they do now. Of course there were obvious problems: how much food do you take? What sort of monsters will you meet? Should you take your spare blue tunic for peace, or your spare red tunic for not peace? And the not-so-obvious problems, like what to do with a wizard who wants to keep an eye on you.

In those days, magic was very important, and territory, to start with, just an extension of the chalk circle you drew around yourself to protect yourself from elementals and the like. It's gone out of fashion now, which is a shame, because sitting in a chalk circle when you feel threatened is a lot better than sitting in the gas oven. Of course people will laugh at you, but people laugh at a great many things, so there's no need to take it personally. Why will it work? It works because the principle of personal space is always the same, whether you're fending off an elemental or someone's bad mood. It's a force field around yourself, and as long as our imagining powers are weak, it's useful to have something physical to remind us.

The training of wizards is a very difficult thing. Wizards have to spend years standing in a chalk circle until they can manage without it. They push out their power bit by bit, first within their hearts, then within their bodies, then within their immediate circle. It is not possible to control the outside of yourself until you have mastered your breathing space. It is not possible to change anything until you understand the substance you wish to change. Of course people mutilate and modify, but these are fallen powers, and to change something you do not understand is the true nature of evil.

For some time Winnet had noticed a strange bird following her, a black thing with huge wings; then for a whole afternoon the bird disappeared. It was that afternoon she saw the sorcerer. The sorcerer stood opposite her, on the other side of a fast flowing stream. She recognized the clothes and would have run away had not the figure called to her above the tumbling.

'I know your name.' And so she stopped, afraid. If this were true she would be trapped. Naming meant power. Adam had named the animals and the animals came at his call.

'I don't believe you,' she shouted back. Then the sorcerer smiled and invited her to cross the stream, so that he could whisper in her ear. She shook her head; the sorcerer's territory must lie across the stream; here at least she was safe.

'You'll never get out of this forest without me,' he warned her, as she picked her way through the mud. Winnet didn't bother to reply. Another night fell, this time bringing rain that gusted the trees, and blew down her shelter. Then she was attacked by an army of water ants, forcing her to move on further into the dark and the forest. By dawn she was exhausted. Her stone jar of food and dry clothes had been lost, and by the bend in the river she realized she had hardly travelled at all. On the other side of the river, smiling gently, she saw the sorcerer.

'I told you,' he said.

This wasn't what Winnet wanted to hear. She sat among some rushes and sulked.

On the other side the sorcerer lit a fire and got out a cooking pot. Winnet sniffed the air, and drew her legs closer. Smelled like pigeon.

'I'm vegetarian,' she yelled, watching his face.

'Oh so am I,' he replied in a pleased tone. 'I'm making adzuki beans and dumplings, there's plenty to spare.'

Winnet was horrified. How could he know? Memories of her grandmother floated towards her; her famous adzuki bean stew; the singing round the fire when the men had gone off to hunt. She hid her nose in her jacket and tried not to breathe.

'Do you like coriander in yours?' the sorcerer called again. 'It's fresh.'

'Yes,' cried Winnet, hoarse and confused, 'but I'm not eating because you'll poison me.'

'My dear!' The sorcerer seemed genuinely shocked.

'How do I know I can trust you?' (Winnet's belly was rumbling.)

'Because I don't know your name. If I did, I'd have spirited you over here already. It's so disappointing dining alone, don't you think?'

Winnet thought it over for a few moments, then made a pact with the sorcerer. She would share his table, then he was to tell her what he wanted, and they'd hold a competition to decide. As a bond he drew her a chalk circle with a tiny gap to step into as she crossed the water. Then he threw the chalk to her on the other side. It was a rough brown pebble, and clutching it tightly she wobbled across the stepping stones, leapt in the circle and closed it behind her.

'French bread or granary?' the sorcerer asked as he passed her a steaming bowl.

For fifteen minutes they chewed in companionable silence, then the sorcerer sighed, tore off another hunk and mopped up his juice. 'There's no pudding I'm afraid. I was planning a custard, but milk's hard to come by round here. Still we'll have coffee, and I'll tell you what I want.'

Winnet's piece of bread stuck in her throat. She started to choke and was forced to let the sorcerer bang her on the back. Perhaps he wanted to chop her up, or turn her into a beast, perhaps he was going to make her marry him. By the time she got her coffee she was rigid with terror.

'What I want,' he began, 'is for you to become my apprentice. The magic arts are dying; the more of us there are, the better. You have gifts, I know that, you can take the message to other places, where even now they hardly know how to draw a chalk circle. I will teach you everything, but I cannot force you, and first you must tell me your name.' He leaned back and looked at Winnet. 'There's just one small thing; unless you tell me your name, you'll never get out of that circle, because I can't release you, and you don't have the power.'

Winnet was speechless with fury. 'You tricked me.'

'Well it is my job you know.'

'All right,' said Winnet after a few moments. 'Here's a deal. If you can guess my name, I'll be yours. If not, you show me how to get out of here, and leave me alone.'

The sorcerer nodded slowly, while Winnet wondered

what fiendish game they must play to decide the
contest. Suddenly the sorcerer looked up.

'Let's play Hang the Man.'

He took out a piece of paper and a fountain pen.
'X,' he started.

'No,' Winnet replied scornfully. 'One to me.'

'You ought to give me a clue,' said the sorcerer,
'after all we aren't using magic arts.'

'All right,' she agreed reluctantly. 'Here's a rhyme.'

'To some my name is almost a bird,
To others a vessel for keeping the curd.'

'And that's all you're getting.'

The sorcerer stood on his head for while, repeating
the chant over and over.

'P,' he said at last.

'Two to me,' trilled Winnet.

Then the magician leapt to his feet crying, 'Your
name is Gannet Barrel.'

'Wrong,' snapped Winnet, 'and I get two points for
that. Next one and I draw in the noose.'

Around nightfall, as Winnet poured them both
another cup of coffee, the sorcerer gave a chuckle.
'I've got it.'

'Oh really?' inquired Winnet. 'Remember I'm free
in about two more goes.'

'Your name is Winnet Stonejar.' And the chalk circle
vanished.

'Oh well,' thought Winnet, scuffing out the fire. 'At
least he can cook.'

The next morning they were standing in a castle with
three ravens staring beakily down from an old flagpost.

'Shadrach, Meshach and Abednego,' the sorcerer introduced. 'You'll get to know which is which, if you'll pardon the pun. Now I'll have to carry you over the doorstep here, or you'll fall asleep. It's all part of the security.' And he picked up Winnet and brought her to a brightly coloured room with a huge hearth blazing at one end.

'Do you like high ceilings?' he asked her, as they perched at either end of the fireplace. 'It's all the same in these old buildings, but you'll get used to it.'

'How long have you been a sorcerer?' Winnet asked, by way of conversation.

'Oh, I can't say,' he replied airily, 'you see I am one in the future too, it's all the same to me.'

'But you can't be,' Winnet argued, 'it's not possible to talk about time like that.'

'Not possible for you my dear, but we're very different.'

This at least was true, so Winnet turned her attention to the room instead.

It had very little furniture, but innumerable cupboards. On the right, by the window, hung an enormous embossed ear trumpet.

'What do you use that for?'

'Well, I'm not always as old as I am now, and when I'm older, I can get a bit deaf. That's so that I can listen to the nightingales at night, when I'm lying on that couch.'

As far as Winnet could see there was no couch. 'What couch?'

'Why that one,' said the sorcerer, surprised. She looked again, and there it was. This was only the beginning of Winnet's adventure at the castle, but as she stayed there, a curious thing happened. She forgot how she had come there, or what she had done before. She believed she had always been in the castle, and that she was the sorcerer's daughter. He told her she was. That she had no mother, but had been specially entrusted to his care by a powerful spirit. Winnet felt this to be true, and besides, where else could she possibly wish to live?

The sorcerer was good to the villagers who lived in clusters under the hills. He taught them music and mathematics and put a strong spell on the crops, so that no one got hungry in winter. Of course, he expected their absolute devotion, but they were glad to give it. Winnet learned to teach the villagers herself, and all went well until one day a stranger came to the settlements. He took lodging at one of the farms, and soon struck up a friendship with Winnet. She invited him to the castle on the day of the great feast.

The great feast was a remembrance and celebration for the village. Each home offered the sorcerer a present, and he gave presents in return, where he thought they were most appropriate.

'Will you give the stranger a present?' Winnet pressed her father, on the morning of the feast.

'What stranger?'

'This one,' pointed Winnet, making him appear. The boy was shocked. A second ago he had been leaning against a tree gazing up at the castle. Now he was standing beside three ravens in a hall so high that the ceiling and the sky were confused. The sorcerer turned to them both and clapped his hands. 'What will be will be, you have already decided his present.' Then gathering his robes about him, Winnet's father was gone.

'I'm frightened,' said the boy.

'No need,' said Winnet, kissing him.

By sundown the hall had filled with people and animals. Some of the animals were gifts to the sorcerer for his own farm, others had just wandered in. By midnight, the wine had caused everyone to forget all but the moment, and the sorcerer was making his customary speech. He promised a good harvest again next year, and good health for his friends. To the young men leaving the village that year, he gave a shield, or a knife, or a bow. To the young women, determined to seek their own living, he gave a falcon, or a dog, or ring. 'Let each protect each according to their needs.' For the sorcerer knew the ways of travellers. Finally his face grew heavy, as he told of a terrible blight come to the land. 'It lies in one of you,' he warned them, watching them ripple with alarm. 'He must be cast out.' And the sorcerer laid his hand on the boy's neck.

'This boy has spoiled my daughter.'

'No,' shouted Winnet, jumping up in alarm. 'He's my friend.'

But no one heard her. They bound the boy and threw him into the darkest room in the deepest part of the castle, where he might have lain forever if Winnet hadn't set him loose by her own arts. 'Now go to him,' she told the boy, as he stood blinking against her torch, 'and deny me. Blame me for whatever you like, you cannot stand by me, for you cannot stand against him.' The boy went pale and wept, but Winnet shoved him up the stairs, and in the morning she heard he had done as she intended.

'Daughter, you have disgraced me,' said the sorcerer, 'and I have no more use for you. You must leave.'

Winnet could not ask forgiveness when she was innocent, but she did ask to stay.

'If you stay, you will stay in the village and care for the goats. I leave you to make up your own mind.' He was gone. Winnet was about to burst into tears when she felt a light pecking at her shoulder. It was Abednego, the raven she loved. He hopped up beside her ear.

'You won't lose your power you know, you'll use it differently, that's all.'

'How do you know?' Winnet sniffed.

'Sorcerers can't take their gifts back, ever, it says so in the book.'

'And what if I stay?'

'You will find yourself destroyed by grief. All you know will be around you, and at the same time far from you. Better to find a new place now.'

Winnet thought about this, while the raven balanced patiently on her shoulder.

'Will you come with me?'

'I can't, I'm bound here, but take this.' The raven flew down and, as far as Winnet could see, started vomiting on the flags. Then he rearranged his feathers, and dropped a rough brown pebble into her hand.

'Thank you,' said Winnet. 'What is it?'

'It's my heart.'

'But it's made of stone.'

'I know,' the raven replied sadly. 'You see I chose to stay, oh, a long time ago, and my heart grew thick with sorrow, and finally set. It will remind you.'

Winnet sat for a moment, at the edge of the fire-place. The raven, struck dumb, could not warn her that her father had crept in, in the shape of a mouse, and was tying an invisible thread around one of her buttons. As Winnet stood up the mouse scuttled away.

She did not notice, and when morning came, she had reached the edge of the forest, and crossed the river.

I had gone back to work at the undertakers, or funeral parlour as the woman and her friend Joe preferred to call it. They paid well and I could always do a bit of extra washing of the cars if I needed more money. Sometimes I had to park the ice-cream van round the back, lay some person out round the front, then get on with my round again. Joe used to joke about dropping the bodies in my freezer when the weather turned warm.

'They'll not notice a bit of raspberry ripple will they?'

The woman was still making wreaths, and much happier since Elysium Fields (that was the name of their business) had won the contract at the posh nursing home just out of town.

'It does mek a difference money does,' she assured me, showing off her new designs. 'They like proper remembrance up there. None of them bloody crosses.'

Joe was doing well too. He'd bought two new vehicles, and was converting the shed into a cold room.

'I don't want to be mowed out with bodies in here,' he said, sweeping his hand round the chapel of rest. 'I mean folks come to pay their last respects, and they don't want any old sod laying with theirs do they? It's only natural to want a bit of privacy.'

'Oh it is, it is,' the woman agreed. 'Don't want 'em lined up like lollies do they?' As far as I could hear, Joe and the woman never answered each other without asking another question. They'd go on for hours while Joe fitted handles and the woman forced wire and flower into an indistinguishable whole. They admired their work.

'Bootiful in't it,' said Joe, 'this brass?'

'Like Heaven's Gates in't it?' the woman returned.

I'd be expected to sit between them nodding wisely and pouring tea. I didn't mind, it was nice to get away from the kids on the ice-cream van. I had a chime that played *Teddy Bears' Picnic*, so they all knew when to come rushing out shouting for orange sticks and ninety-nines. The important thing about the chime was to wind it up, otherwise it groaned through the tune so slowly that Joe once offered to buy it for his vehicles. On the other hand if you wound it up too much, it sounded like that Western music they play when the cavalry comes chasing down the hill. 'It's bloody Trickett's,' people said when I got it wrong, 'bugger off.' They were fickle. They ran across the alley to Birtwistle's, the last horse-drawn ice-cream cart. Birtwistle was at least eighty and his horse had the droop. Folks said no one knew what went into his mixing pail, and no one ever asked. It tasted good though. He didn't do anything fancy, just cornets and wafers, covered in strawberry syrup. He called it blood. When I was little, we always bought from him, because there was a bonus. We were the round on his way home, and for the whole day people fed the horse odds and ends, so that by the time it came steaming up the hill, shit was pouring out the back. My mother heard the whistle, and shoving a ten-shilling note in one hand and a shovel in the other, sent me out for two wafers, one cornet, and whatever I could carry off the cobbles. The horse stamped and blew and usually dropped a bit more for me, once I'd bought the ice-creams.

'Grand,' beamed my mother as I tottered down the lobby trying not to slop. 'Go and dig it in to me lettuces.' Then we'd sit content with our bloody wafers.

There was a romance about Birtwistle's that Trickett's never had. When Elysium Fields arranged a wake for someone, they always used Birtwistle's for the dessert.

'It's quality in't it?' the woman said.

The wakes were very fine. Always the best. Since the nursing home contract they had included a starter, usually prawn cocktail from Molly's Seafoods. For the main course you could choose between turkey roll, beef slices, or hot quiche. The quiche was thought to be a bit daring at first, but had become very popular.

'You need a bit of fancy don't you?' the woman told me, when I went to print the menu.

On Saturday, as I drove the ice-cream van round Lower Fold, I saw a crowd of people milling outside the end terrace. The end terrace was Elsie's house. I tried to drive straight there, but somebody wanted a lolly, then somebody wanted a wafer, and my hands shook and I couldn't make the scoops.

'Bit sloppy, you,' a fat woman complained.

'Have a free choc-ice,' I said, throwing it at her, then as she stood staring, hands on hips, with her choc-ice poking out of her pinny pocket, I roared the engine and bounced down the cobbles. No one took any notice of me, parking the van, or getting out, or pushing through to Elsie's door. In the parlour were Mrs White, the pastor and my mother. No Elsie.

'What's happening?' I demanded.

They glanced at me, but carried on discussing in

low voices. I caught the words 'funeral arrangements'.
Then I grabbed my mother by her coat sleeve.

'Will you tell me what's going on?'

She brushed her coat sleeve. 'Elsie's dead.'

The pastor came up to me. 'Go home please
Jeanette.' His voice was very quiet.

'And where do you suppose that is?' I shot back
at him. He never flinched, just took me by the arm,
and led me into the lobby.

'We haven't really talked much have we?' he asked.

I didn't answer, just looked at the floor, wanting
not to cry.

'You should have trusted me.' His voice was soft.

'What are you afraid of?' I suddenly wanted to know.

He smiled. 'I am afraid of Hell, of eternal damnation.'

'So what's so awful about me?'

Then he lost his temper, as only a soft-voiced man
can. 'You made an immoral proposition that cannot
be countenanced.'

'It takes two you know,' I thought it fair to remind
him.

'She was confused by you, you used your power
over her, it wasn't her, it was you.'

'She loved me.' As soon as I had said this I felt he
would kill me if he could.

'She did not love you.'

'Is that what she said?'

'She told me herself.'

I leaned on the wall, two palms flat, breathing out.
There are different kinds of treachery, but betrayal is
betrayal wherever you find it. No, he wouldn't kill
me, soft-voiced men do not kill, they are clever. Their
kind of violence leaves no visible mark. He led me

to the door, and I stumbled towards the ice-cream van. 'Here she is.' I heard a shout and saw that all the people bundled round Elsie's were forming a queue outside my window. The first one took out her purse.

'Two wafers luv. Did you know her in there? I knew her by sight.' Then she turned to her friend. 'We knew her by sight didn't we?' I passed them the wafers.

The women who came next were all together and gossiping.

'She felt no pain, she just slipped over in the night, two raspberries and one vanilla please luv, Betty hasn't made up her mind yet, yet it were the best way, she were old you know, she couldn't look after herself any more.'

'Do you want anything else?' I asked them.

'Yes,' Betty raised her voice, 'a ninety-nine for me, I'm not paying.' And they burst out laughing. 'Get a move on,' ordered the woman who was paying, 'I've me kids at home.'

At last they'd all gone, but just as I dumped my sticky scoops into the cloudy cleaning jar, I saw Mrs White crossing the road towards me. She was sniffling into a handkerchief.

'Making money out of the dead,' she whimpered through the window. 'The pastor can't believe it.'

'It's not holy is it?' I said to her.

'No it's not, but you'll pay the price, and it'll be more than a cornet.'

'I expect so,' I said, hoping she'd go away, but she just leaned on the window shelf, sobbing so much that I had to wipe her up with a dishcloth.

'When's the funeral?' I asked, by way of conversation.

'You can't come, it's for the holy.'

'I don't want to come, oh go away.' I went to the wheel, and Mrs White muttered something at me, then ran back across the road.

So I went on as usual, not thinking at all, past Woodnook Baptist church, then up the long hill to Fern Gore, where the ice-cream works was. 'I need a couple of days off,' I told them. 'It won't happen again.' They weren't pleased, school holidays were a busy time, but I worked hard, and made good money, so they let me go.

When Winnet crossed the river, she found herself in a part of the forest that looked the same but smelt different. Since she had no idea where she was going, she decided almost anywhere would do, and set off down the most obvious path. Soon she ran out of food and spare clothes, then homesickness struck her, and she lay unable to walk for many days. A woman travelling in the forest found her body, and by means of herbs revived her. This woman knew nothing of the magic arts, but she understood the different kinds of sorrow and their effects. Winnet went with her, back to her village, where the people made her welcome and gave her work for a living. They had heard of Winnet's father, believed him mad and dangerous, and so Winnet never spoke of her own powers, and never used them. The woman tried to teach Winnet her language, and Winnet learned the words but not the language. Certain constructions baffled her, and in an argument they could always be used against her, because she could not use them in return. But mostly this didn't happen. The villagers were simple and kind, not questioning the world. They didn't expect Winnet to talk very much. Winnet wanted to talk. She had left her school and her followers far behind, she wanted to talk about the nature of the world, why it was there at all, and what they were all doing on it. Yet at the same time she knew her old world had much in it that was wrong. If she talked about it, good and bad, they would think her mad, and then she would have no one. She had to pretend she was just like them, and when she made a mistake, they smiled and remembered she was foreign. Winnet had heard that there was a beautiful city, a long way off, with buildings that ran up to the sky. It was an ancient city, guarded by tigers. No one in her village had been there, but all of them knew about it, and most held it in awe. The city dwellers didn't sow or toil, they thought about the world. Winnet lay awake many nights, trying to imagine what such a place would really be like. If only she could get there, she felt sure she'd be safe. When she told the villagers her plan, they laughed, and told her to think about other things, but Winnet could think about nothing else, and she set her mind to making it happen.

In town, the following morning, I saw Joe. He waved and hurried up to me.

'We've got one of yours in the parlour. Go over and have a look.' I knew he meant Elsie. This was my last chance. None of the church remembered that I helped out at Elysium Fields. In the meantime, I had a letter to write, so waited until evening before walking across town, besides, there was the prayer meeting at church that night, so I'd be unlikely to meet anyone.

'Oh, it's you is it?' the woman looked up as I arrived. 'Is Joe there?'

'Yes it's me, and no, Joe isn't, he'll be at the allotment won't he?'

'Oh yes, digging up veg for the funeral supper. I forgot.' The woman was weaving fern and hyacinths into a cross. 'Look what I'm doing for them, another bloody cross.' She slapped it down in a temper. 'Let's have a drink of tea.' I passed by Elsie's coffin on my way to the little kitchen, but I didn't look in, I wanted to wait until they'd gone home. It felt peaceful though.

'Fetch them Bourbons,' the woman yelled.

We sat in the sun for half an hour or so, enjoying the warm and the tea.

'Best thing to come out of France,' the woman declared, biting her Bourbon.

'What about quiche?' I reminded her.

'Right, that's right,' she nodded. 'They do know about food don't they?' And she started to tell me some recipes she'd seen in a book in the library, and the time she'd sailed across the Channel to Dieppe. She wouldn't go again, no, it was too far, though she'd like to see the Eiffel Tower. She'd heard it had been built by acrobats, and that a troupe of trained monkeys had put up the last and highest girders. Her own grandmother had seen a picture of it, and a scale model in the Great Exhibition. She'd a picture of her grandmother seeing a picture of it. Did I want to travel? No I didn't, well she could understand that, what with so much to do at home. Then she said she thought it depended on your reincarnation. I wasn't to tell anyone she thought this. It was in confidence. She said she'd often wondered why she wanted to do some things and not do other things at all. Well, it was obvious with some things, but for others, there was no reason there. She'd spent a long time puzzling it out, then she thought that what you'd done in a past life you didn't need to do again, and what you had to do in the future, you wouldn't be ready to do now.

'It's like building blocks in't it?'

This, she felt, explained why I didn't want to travel. Just then Joe drove up, and the woman went to make a fresh pot of tea. He opened the back of the vehicle.

'I got pots, and beets and tomatoes and lettuces, an sum of them pea pods. That should do. They're having turkey roll with vanilla ice-cream afterwards.'

'When is it?'

'Tomorrow at twelve o'clock. We'd best sweep out the vehicle first though. There's enough soil where she's going in't there?'

The woman came out with the tea. She was upset because Joe had promised to take her to the pictures that night to see Gary Cooper. Now he was talking about washing the vehicle. She spilt his tea into the saucer, and hid the packet of Bourbons under her fern. I didn't want her to be miserable, so I offered to clean out the vehicle, and give it a polish.

'Can you put it in't garage?' asked Joe, doubtful.

'Course she can,' snapped the woman, 'she drives that bloody ice-cream van enough.'

Joe nodded and looked at his watch.

'All right then, let's get you home for a wash.' The woman got up to fetch her helmet – Joe didn't wear one – then they got on to the little scooter and weaved down the lane. I waited a while, then slowly found the bucket and leather, and cleaned the vehicle. I wanted Elsie to have the best. It was dark by the time I eased it into the garage. I washed my hands and went into the parlour; just a few lights were burning, enough to see Elsie. She was laid out in her Sunday best, with her hymnbook next to her. The hymnbook was full of Elsie's markings, telling her what key to play in. I wondered what they'd done with her accordion. There was a stool made for looking into the coffins, the right height, so that you didn't have to stand. Joe was always sensitive about these things; he'd let you stay the night if you wanted to, though it wasn't common practice.

I talked to Elsie for a long time about the way I felt, and the letter I'd written. It was dawn before I went home.

Downstairs, the telephone was ringing. I wanted to stay asleep, but the telephone went on ringing. It was Joe. He was in a panic. Would I come and do the meal, cook it and serve it? He had to drive the vehicle and see to the coffin. The woman had fallen off the scooter on the way home from the Gary Cooper film. She hadn't broken anything, but she needed to stay in bed for a few days. She'd just managed to finish the wreath. I tried to tell Joe what would happen if I showed up at the funeral.

'It's all right,' he said, 'I'll not miss their custom, they can go to gloomy Alf next time.' Alf ran a very different kind of establishment, with set burials at set prices.

'Like a bloody Chinese takeaway,' Joe scoffed.

So I agreed, took some clothes to change into, and went off to cook turkey roll for twenty.

I kept out of sight until the cortège had set off, then rushed to lay the table. I reckoned I could set out the prawn cocktail, and leave them to help themselves to veg, once they'd got a plate of turkey each. Forty-five minutes later they were back, so I ran out with the red hot tureens of steaming veg and fixed them all along the table. Now, Joe could hand out the plates, and we might get away with it. It went well, until the ice-cream. The portions were standing by on the tray; Joe had promised to carry them through, then get everyone to leave the table, for coffee and cake in the parlour, so I could clear up. Suddenly the vicar from the cemetery stood up, and motioned Joe over to the door. Joe looked panic-stricken then came over to me, where I was peeping behind the kitchen window.

'You'll have to do the ice-cream. He wants to talk to me.'

'But Joe . . .' I was terrified, and he had already gone.

I picked up the first tray and tried to make my face look different.

'Vanilla?' I asked Mrs White, plonking it down in front of her.

'Vanilla, Pastor?' I asked, spilling some of it.

'Vanilla May? Vanilla Alice?' And I vanilla'd my way down the line until I came to my mother. She was staring at me, with her mouth a little bit open.

'You?' and her pearls quivered against her throat.

'Me. Vanilla?'

Elsie's relatives from Morecambe thought we'd gone mad. The pastor stood up.

'Where's Mr Ramsbottom? Is this a sick joke?'

'The woman's ill,' I explained, 'I'm helping out.'

'Have you no shame?'

'Not really.'

The pastor motioned to the flock. 'We won't stay to be mocked any longer.'

'Oh she's a demon your daughter,' wailed Mrs White, holding on to the pastor's arm.

'She's no daughter of mine,' snapped back my mother, head high, leading the way out.

And they left, and so the relatives from Morecambe had seconds, and two pieces of Battenburg. When Joe came back he just shook his head, said they were all mad, and that I was well out of it. He was right, but I was lonely. As I washed up in the kitchen thinking it over, I felt someone standing behind me.

It was Miss Jewsbury.

'You weren't at the meal,' was all I could think of to say.

'No, I didn't want that. I wanted to see Elsie off, that's all. I know her cousin from Morecambe.' I didn't reply, and she looked awkward. 'How are you then?'

'Oh fine,' I told her, 'I can make some money, and I have a plan for next year.'

She was the first person I'd confided in, apart from Elsie. She seemed pleased, told me it was a good idea, that she should have done it herself. 'Things get in the way,' she said, 'that's what's sad about life.' Then suddenly, 'Will you come and see me in my flat?'

'No,' I answered slowly, 'I can't do that.'

She gathered her bags and her gloves. 'Well if you change your mind, or if you need money, I'm in the directory.' She turned away, and I heard her heels for a long time. I don't know why I didn't thank her, or even say goodbye.

That was the last time I worked for the Elysium

Fields on a regular basis. I had finished school and been offered a full-time job in a mental hospital. It wasn't something I would have chosen normally, but it had a distinct advantage over other jobs, because I could live in. A room of my own, at least.

'She'll not like, will she?' the woman said to Joe.

'How can she?' Joe replied, 'All them lunatics.'

But I went, nevertheless, comforting myself with my plan.

Winnet tried to imagine what the city might be like. Some of her village said it was made of crystal, others, that it had been spun from a web. Some called it a nonsense, and told her she'd still be unhappy even if she managed to find it. She thought how everyone must be strong and healthy. She thought of their compassion and wisdom. In a place where truth mattered, no one would betray her, and so her courage grew, and with it, her determination. She found a map rolled up round a broom handle; the map showed the forest, and the edges of the forest where the towns began. She found the river, placid and shrunk, but growing to a huge mouth where she had once lived; the river belted the sacred city, and splitting itself like a cut worm, flowed variously into the sea. Winnet had never sailed on the sea. She had known the sea only as it came to the shore, known it only in connection with the land. She was afraid of it, though she knew the faithful have made miracles from coracles. The easiest way to the city was out into the sea, then back up the river again. The only other way was through the deepest forest, down a part of the river that looked like a tunnel. The waters there were brackish, she could not hope to navigate them, as they lost themselves in a thick tree-dark that lasted long after the night. She must find a boat and sail in it. No guarantee of shore. Only a conviction that what she wanted could exist, if she dared to find it.

Winnet studied the ways of boat builders; how they turned and trimmed the hull for speed, and fattened the stern for steadiness. She learned the geometry of a sail. The blind man who taught her said rope was like a dog, rough and dependable. Warm and scratchy like a dog's coat, and brown and needing to be handled right. She learned to handle everything like it was alive. It was alive, he told her, and it worked better if you knew it. He told her it was Wu li: principles of organic energy. She didn't understand, but she felt it moving; the rich black tar and the tight thread bound round the stem of her oars. When the stones are hot, he said, they sing, and he gave her a singing stone for her journey.

Soon it was Winnet's last night at the village. She decided to sleep outside, where she could sniff and sense the earth she was leaving. The wind blew and it didn't seem important, but tomorrow when the wind blew, it would be important. All the familiar things were getting different meanings. In the night, Winnet had a dream.

She dreamed her eyebrows became two bridges that ran to a bore-hole between her eyes. The hole has no cover, and a spiral staircase starts, and runs down and down into the gut. She must follow it if she wants to know the extent of her territory. She must pass through the blood and bones that swill round the bottom step, before she can squat on the top step, in the huge space under her skin. Then she finds a roundabout horse, and that gives her a chance to look at things more than once, and she thinks she doesn't change anything as she looks, but she must, because every time she goes round, the same things are different. She's getting dizzy, if she doesn't jump she'll fall off.

When Winnet wakes up, there's a light rain, and she must move quickly. She's crying and the blind man, touching her, tells her not to worry about being afraid. She rows out to the sea, and stores her boat for a day, until she gets used to the salt taste and how big it all is. The need for the city fastens her heart to her mind. She will get in her boat and sail to the other side. The sail is pulling and the sun is out. Now there is nothing about her but water. One thing is certain; she can't go back.

'When did you last see your mother?' someone asked me. Someone who was walking with me in the city. I didn't want to tell her; I thought in this city, a past was precisely that. Past. Why do I have to remember? In the old world, anyone could be a new creation, the past was washed away. Why should the new world be so inquisitive?

'Don't you ever think of going back?'

Silly question. There are threads that help you find your way back, and there are threads that intend to bring you back. Mind turns to the pull, it's hard to pull away. I'm always thinking of going back. When Lot's wife looked over her shoulder, she turned into a pillar of salt. Pillars hold things up, and salt keeps things clean, but it's a poor exchange for losing your self. People do go back, but they don't survive, because two realities are claiming them at the same time. Such things are too much. You can salt your heart, or kill your heart, or you can choose between the two realities. There is much pain here. Some people think you can have your cake and eat it. The cake goes mouldy and they choke on what's left. Going back after a long time will make you mad, because the people you left behind do not like to think of you changed, will treat you as they always did, accuse you of being indifferent, when you are only different.

'When did you last see your mother?'

I don't know how to answer. I know what I think, but words in the head are like voices under water. They are distorted. Hearing the words as they hit the surface is sensitive work. You will have to be a bank robber and listen and listen to the little clicks before you can open the safe.

'What would have happened if you had stayed?'

I could have been a priest instead of a prophet. The priest has a book with the words set out. Old words, known words, words of power. Words that are always on the surface. Words for every occasion. The words work. They do what they're supposed to do; comfort and discipline. The prophet has no book. The prophet is a voice that cries in the wilderness, full of sounds that do not always set into meaning. The prophets cry out because they are troubled by demons.

This ancient city is made of stone and stone walls that have not fallen yet. Like paradise it is bounded by rivers, and contains fabulous beasts. Most of them have heads. If you drink from the wells, and there are many, you might live forever, but there is no guarantee you will live forever as you are. You might mutate. The waters might not agree with you. They don't tell

you this. I came to this city to escape. This city is full
of towers to climb and climb, and to climb faster and
faster, marvelling at the design and dreaming of the
view from the top. At the top there is a keen wind
and everything is so far away it's impossible to say
what is what. There is no one to discuss it with. Cats
can count on the fire brigade, and Rapunzel was lucky
with her hair. Wouldn't it be nice to sit on the ground
again? I came to this city to escape.

If the demons lie within they travel with you.

Everyone thinks their own situation most tragic. I
am no exception.

As I change from the inter-city to the local line, I
notice something odd. This is a busy station, but there
are hardly any people, and very little noise. It's muffled,
like the universe has been gagged. What's going on?
A hand at my shoulder.

'Last train luv.' I search for the clock. It's only half-
past eight.

The voice sees my confusion. 'Snow luv, lines are
clogged.' What is he talking about? I travel just a few
hundred miles and I am cut off. I feel suspicious. I
am in the sphere of enchantment and anything is
possible. Right now though, I must get on to this
train. My carriage is already occupied by a sighing
man. I haven't brought gloves, and the luggage
hammock above me has rotted.

'Don't put yer bags in the aisle luv,' the ticket clipper
scolds.

We shunt off and I make a porthole in the fug.
Beyond the window there must be three feet of snow.
The tracks are covered and the sidings are packed

high. I haven't brought my wellingtons. The sighing
man turns into a muttering man until we reach our
first station. We don't stay long, then there is an ear-
piercing shriek. The train stammers and halts, jerks a
few more feet, then different feet come running down
the aisle. The clipper man and the guard and the
muttering man drag behind them. The shrieking does
not stop. I stick my head out of the door and see a
great black bundle being tugged on to the train.
Suddenly the bundle pops through, and we are off
again. As I move back to my seat, I notice the bundle
coming down the train towards me. 'Bloody hell,
bloody hell, bloody hell,' it chants. 'Don't give a body
time to climb on. Bloody hell, and me with a bad
heart.' The woman had got stuck in the door.

There are three of us now; the bundle chanting
her complaint round a fat cheese sandwich, one fat
hand clasping a thermos like a long lost friend; the
muttering man singing a ditty about love and the lack
of it; and me, with a copy of *Middlemarch* under my
pullover. It is not the one thing nor the other that
leads to madness, but the space in between them.

'Well, here we are,' I thought, as the train sidled up
to what used to be a station. In the old days it had
a model of the *Queen Mary*, and a waiting room and
a machine full of Fry's Five Boys. I went to Liverpool
from here once, wearing a hat that looked like a tea
cosy. Elsie knitted it for me; she called it my Helmet
of Salvation.

The wind blew, and my shoes got darker and damp
as I slithered past the town hall, Christmas pine radiant,
crib courtesy of the Salvation Army. It had begun to

snow again as I reached the bottom of our long stretchy street. The hill at the top looked like the bundle on the train. 'Ten blocks, twenty street-lamps.' I counted automatically. Soon be there. I wished I'd brought gloves. The last few flags and suddenly I'm outside my front door again. The parlour has a leaded window, so no one can see inside properly. I can see shapes though, and I can hear what sounds like *Hark the Herald Angels Sing*; it sounds like it, but in the background there is the distinct rhythm of a samba. I hover, then, mustering all my hormones, push open the front door. The lobby is lit, the reindeer shoehorn still hangs by the barometer, though the wallpaper no longer does. I will go into the parlour and hope for the best. In the parlour I find my mother sitting in front of what is best described as a contraption. More interestingly, she is playing it.

'Hello Mum, it's me.' I put down my bag and waited. She swivelled round on her stool, waving a piece of sheet music. The cover said 'Glad Tidings'.

'Come and look at this, it's specially for the electronic organ,' and she spun back again, rippling the keys.

'What have you done with the piano?'

'Oh, I've gone all electronic now. I like to keep up with the world.'

I went over to inspect the contraption. It was enormous, with a great flourish of a music stand on the top. There were two keyboards, and a row of different coloured knobs and buttons, with things like 'Spinet', and 'Xylophone' printed on them.

'Listen to this spinet,' my mother commanded, and tinkled out the first verse of *In the Bleak Mid-Winter*.

'It's very atmospheric,' I had to admit.

'Oh it's more than that, I'll show you.' And for the next half-hour she demonstrated the contraption. *We Three Kings* with and without snare. *We Three Kings* with and without flugel horn and bass ensemble. She could play pop too, guitar and up tempo beat. 'For the youth meetings,' she explained. 'We're going to get a band going, just like The Joystrings.' She switched it off, then stood back so that we could both admire it. 'The stool comes with it.' She pointed at the sculpture of plush and melamine. 'And you get a bound copy of your favourite music book. Course, I had *The Redemption Hymnal* done, see.' They had bound it in calfette, with gold leaf lettering, and my mother's initials on the spine. I nodded and asked if we could have a cup of tea.

'Did you get it from the Society for the Lost?' I asked her, thinking she might even have designed the accessories. For a moment she didn't answer, then I saw she was blushing. She told me that the Society had been disbanded, that there had been corruption at the Morecambe guest house, and that the Rev. Bone was a broken man. It appeared that most of the money put aside for the fishermen's missions had gone to pay the secretary's gambling debts; the profits from my mother's memberships and sales of religious accoutrements had gone to pay his wife maintenance. His estranged wife. The woman he lived with was his girlfriend.

'Pompadour,' spat my mother. 'Living in sin with his pompadour.'

When it was discovered that the Society was on the verge of bankruptcy, my mother composed a letter to her vast battery of members, asking for funds, and warning them that the Society would not be present for much longer. The response had been over-whelming; postal orders began to arrive by the next delivery accompanied by notes of thanks for all the happiness through the years. 'I carry my wipe-clean copy of Revelations everywhere,' wrote one woman. Finally my mother sold off all the remaining copies of *The Jim Reeves Devotional Selection* at half-price. They cleared their debts, with enough over for the Rev. Bone to take a short holiday in Colwyn Bay.

At the Morecambe guest house reports of watered-down soup and unchanged towels caused an investigation by the health authorities. The place had slipped into disrepair, and was ordered to clean up or close down. This was bad enough, but my mother had discovered an advert from them in the *Psychic Weekly* offering those recently bereaved the services of 'Morecambe's most famous medium'. The guest house had started holding seances every Friday in the billiard room. You had to pay extra, and miss your evening meal, because the medium didn't like to work with full stomachs. My mother was so upset that she submitted a long piece on devilry to the *Band of Hope* review. She gave it to me to read for bedtime.

'Have you got enough to keep you occupied?' I asked her anxiously.

'I told you I'd gone electronic, well it doesn't stop in the parlour.' She was mysterious and wouldn't tell me anymore. We spoke for a while of what I was doing and why. No detail, just enough to make both of us feel like we were making an effort.

'Your cousin's in the police force now,' she said brightly.

'That's nice.'

'Yes, she's got a young man' (she's deliberately not looking at me).

'That's nice.'

'She asks after you.'

'Well just tell her I'm not dead, then she won't waste money on a wreath.' I decided it was time I went to bed. 'Don't forget this,' chirped my mother, tossing her article after me.

Sir Perceval came to a glorious castle built of mountain rock and set upon the side of a hill. As he approached the drawbridge, it lowered towards him and he saw trout swimming in the moat. His horse is weary. Sir Perceval dismounts and they walk across the water together. On either side of the ramparts stands a dwarf, fully armed. They greet the knight, tell him he is welcome, tell him there is meat inside. One takes the horse, while the other leads the way. Sir Perceval finds himself in a room made entirely of oak. The dwarf bids him rest till sundown. Sir Perceval curses himself for leaving the Round Table, leaving the king, and the king's sorrowing face. On his last night at Camelot, he found Arthur walking in the garden, and Arthur had cried like a child, and said there was nothing. The king had given him a string of bells for his horse. On the first day and the second day and the third day, Perceval could have turned back, he was still within the sphere of Merlin. On the fourth day, the woods were wild and forlorn, and he did not know where he was, or even what had driven him there. Now Sir Perceval lay on the bed and fell asleep.

He dreamed of that supper time, when there was a great cracking and crying of thunder and in the midst of the blast entered a sunbeam seven times brighter than the day. Each of them saw the other as they had never seen before, and every man was struck dumb. Then into the hall came the Holy Grail covered with white samite. They had vowed there and then to seek it, and not to rest until they had obtained a full view of it, and Arthur had sat silent looking out of the window.

When Perceval awoke, the sun was sinking. He must wash and greet his host. He would speak of the Grail, but not of his reason for seeking it. He had seen the vision of perfect heroism and, for a fleeting moment, the vision of perfect peace. He sought it again, to balance him. He was a warrior who longed to grow herbs.

My mother woke me with a cup of hot chocolate and a shopping list. I was to go down town for her; she had to write to Pastor Spratt. The snow had worsened, so that my first stop had to be the Army and Navy for a pair of wellingtons. Feeling stouter, I decided to visit Mrs Arkwright at her vermin shop. The bell tinkled and she raised her eyes from the powder she was bagging. It took her almost five minutes to recognise me, then she leaned over the counter and banged me on the shoulder. 'Hello,' I said, brushing off the flea powder. 'How are you?'

'Sick and fed up,' she started to put on her coat. 'You're old enough for a drink in the Cock and Whistle now aren't you?' I nodded and she put her sign on the door, and escorted me into the pub. My mother had always told me that the Cock and Whistle was a den of thieves and tax collectors. Now that I saw it for the first time, it wasn't nearly so exciting. It had a lino floor and a few withered-up old men at the bar. Mrs Arkwright marched me into the snug, and ordered two halves of mild. 'Well,' she said, 'I thought you'd buggered off for good.'

'I'm just here for Christmas.'

She sniffed. 'Well more fool you. It's a bloody dust hole this place, dead.'

'Is business bad?'

'Bloody awful. It's that new-fangled central heating. You can't have it fitted without a damp course, and it clears all the bugs at the same time. I've complained, and I've tried to get compensation, but they say it's progress, and I should concentrate on pet care.'

'Can't you do that?'

Mrs Arkwright banged the table. 'No I bloody can't, they all want to act posh round here now, don't want to be seen in no vermin shop. Besides, you know I can't stand them poodles. I'm not running a flaming poodle parlour.'

I asked her when all this had started, and why.

'Bathrooms,' she said darkly. 'Bathrooms did it.' It appeared that the council had finally got round to recognising that the houses on the Factory Bottoms were less than desirable. They had made available large sums of money for basic improvements. Every back-to-back terrace had been granted a bathroom.

'After bathrooms they want central heating and poodles,' Mrs Arkwright thundered on. 'We all know what central heating does to you. Dry's up yer natural juices dun't it?' She felt very bitter, after the way she'd protected the community for so many years. She'd invested in all the latest pesticides, given advice at all hours, and worked hard at keeping up to date with foreign imports.

'There's not a bug anywhere I can't recognise,' she told me proudly.

'What are you going to do?'

She glanced at me, then glanced around, then put her finger to her lips. I had to promise not to breathe a word. She had some savings, and she'd saved all her winnings on the bingo. She was going to emigrate.

I was fascinated. She'd never been further than Blackpool in her life.

'Where are you going?'

'Torremolinos.'

'What?'

'Yes, I've had the booklets, and I've found one of them villas. I'm going to sell soft toys to tourists. They'll be glad to buy from someone that speaks English.' I thought about the cost of buying a villa, the flight, the stock, the money to live on, while she found her feet. She was burbling on about how she'd been learning Spanish for six months out of a book and at a night class in Rishton twice a week.

'Have you got enough money?' I had to ask.

'Not quite. That's why I have to burn down me shop.' She watched me closely, then reminded me I had promised not to say a word. 'If you give me your address, I'll send you a copy of the write-up in the paper.'

She had it all worked out: slow-burning fuse, lots of inflammables. She'd set it for her night class so that she'd be well out of the way. She didn't want her furniture anyway, and she would buy new clothes. She'd put her documents and valuables in a bank deposit. Still, she wasn't doing anything till after Christmas.

'I don't want to drag firemen away from their families.'

We drank up, and I left her as I had found her, bagging flea powder.

I bought the mince and the onions and found that Trickett's snack bar was still in the same place serving the same things. Betty still had the tape round her spectacles, all these years after Mona had dropped her beefburgers on top of them. She didn't know who I was, and I didn't want to talk about it. I was beginning to wonder if I'd ever been anywhere. My mother was treating me like she always had; had she noticed my absence? Did she even remember why I'd left? I have a theory that every time you make an important choice, the part of you left behind continues the other life you could have had. Some people's emanations are very strong, some people create themselves afresh outside of their own body. This is not fancy. If a potter has an idea, she makes it into a pot, and it exists beyond her, in its own separate life. She uses a physical substance to display her thoughts. If I use a metaphysical substance to display my thoughts, I might be anywhere at one time, influencing a number of different things, just as the potter and her pottery can exert influence in different places. There's a chance that I'm not here at all, that all the parts of me, running along all the choices I did and didn't make, for a moment brush against each other. That I am still an evangelist in the North, as well as the person who ran away. Perhaps for a while these two selves have become confused. I have not gone forward or back in time, but across in time, to something I might have been, playing itself out.

'You've spilt your tea,' said Betty indignantly. So I paid her double and left.

I didn't go straight home, I went up on to the hill. No one else was there, with the weather like this. If I still lived there, I'd be indoors too. It's a visitor's privilege to be foolish. Right to the top I climbed, where I could watch the circling snow fill up the town till it blotted it out. All the black blotted out. I could have made a very impressive sermon . . . 'My sins like a cloud hung over me, he blotted them out when he set me free . . .' that sort of thing. But where was God now, with heaven full of astronauts, and the Lord overthrown? I miss God. I miss the company of someone utterly loyal. I still don't think of God as my betrayer. The servants of God, yes, but servants by their very nature betray. I miss God who was my friend. I don't even know if God exists, but I do know that if God is your emotional role model, very few human relationships will match up to it. I have an idea that one day it might be possible, I thought once it had become possible, and that glimpse has set me wandering, trying to find the balance between earth and sky. If the servants hadn't rushed in and parted us, I might have been disappointed, might have snatched off the white samite to find a bowl of soup. As it is, I can't settle, I want someone who is fierce and will love me until death and know that love is as strong as death, and be on my side for ever and ever. I want someone who will destroy and be destroyed by me. There are many forms of love and affection, some people can spend their whole lives together without knowing each other's names. Naming is a difficult and time-consuming process; it concerns essences, and it means power. But on the wild nights who can call you home? Only the one who knows your name. Romantic love has been diluted into paperback form and has sold thousands and millions of copies. Somewhere it is still in the original, written on tablets of stone. I would cross seas and suffer sunstroke and give away all I have, but not for a man, because they want to be the destroyer and never be destroyed. That is why they are unfit for romantic love. There are exceptions and I hope they are happy.

The unknownness of my needs frightens me. I do not know how huge they are, or how high they are, I only know that they are not being met. If you want to find out the circumference of an oil drop, you can use lycopodium powder. That's what I'll find. A tub of lycopodium powder, and I will sprinkle it on to my needs and find out how large they are. Then when I meet someone I can write up the experiment and show them what they have to take on. Except they might have a growth rate I can't measure, or they might mutate, or even disappear. One thing I am certain of, I do not want to be betrayed, but that's quite hard to say, casually, at the beginning of a relationship. It's not a word people use very often, which confuses me, because there are different kinds of infidelity, but betrayal is betrayal wherever you find it. By betrayal, I mean promising to be on your side, then being on somebody else's.

Standing on the side of the hill, just where it slopes into the quarry, it's possible to see where Melanie used to live. I met her by accident, during the second year that I was away from home; she was pushing a pram. If she had been serene to the point of bovine before, she was now almost vegetable. I kept looking at her, and wondering how we ever had a relationship; yet when she first left me, I thought I had blood poisoning. I couldn't forget her. Now she seemed to have forgotten everything. It made me want to shake her, to pull off all my clothes in the middle of the street and yell, 'Remember this body?' Time is a great deadener; people forget, get bored, grow old, go away. She said that not much had happened between us anyway, historically speaking. But history is a string full of knots, the best you can do is admire it, and maybe knot it up a bit more. History is a hammock for swinging and a game for playing. A cat's cradle. She said those sorts of feelings were dead, the feelings she once had for me. There is a certain seductiveness about dead things. You can ill treat, alter and recolour what's dead. It won't complain. Then she laughed and said we probably saw what had happened very differently anyway . . . She laughed again, and said that the way I saw it would make a good story, her vision was just the history, the nothing-at-all facts. She said she hoped I hadn't kept any letters, silly to hang on to things that had no meaning. As though letters and photos made it more real, more dangerous. I told her I didn't need her letters to remember what had happened. Then she looked vague and started to discuss the weather and the roadworks and the soaring price of baby food.

She asked me what I was doing, and I longed to say I was sacrificing infants on top of Pendle Hill or dabbling in the white slave trade. Anything to make her angry. Still, in her terms, she was happy. They had stopped eating meat, and she was pregnant again, and so on. She had even started writing to my mother. They had worked together on the town's first mission for coloured people. My mother had emptied her War Cupboard of tinned pineapple, because she thought that's what they ate. She had also gone round collecting blankets so that they wouldn't be cold. When the first coloured pastor came to her house, she had tried to explain to him the significance of parsley sauce. Later she found he had lived most of his life in Hull. Melanie, still waiting for her missionary posting, had dealt with all this as best she could, but she was out of her depth. And so, for the length of the mission, everyone had to eat gammon with pineapple, pineapple upside-down cake, chicken in pineapple sauce, pineapple chunks, pineapple slice. 'After all,' said my mother philosophically, 'oranges are not the only fruit.'

It was getting dark as I came down the hill, swirls of snow sticking to my face. I thought about the dog and was suddenly very sad; sad for her death, for my death, for all the inevitable dying that comes with change. There's no choice that doesn't mean a loss. But the dog was buried in the clean earth, and the things I had buried were exhuming themselves; clammy fears and dangerous thoughts and the shadows I had put away for a more convenient time. I could not put them away forever, there is always a day of reckoning. But not all dark places need light, I have to remember that.

When I got in, my mother was wearing a pair of headphones and jotting something down on a piece of paper. In front of her was a large radio set. I tapped her on the shoulder.

'You could have given me a heart attack,' she snapped, switching knobs up and down. 'I can't talk now, I'm receiving.'

'Receiving what?'

'My reports.' And she jammed on her headphones and started scribbling again. It was well over an hour before I could get any sense out of her. We sat together with a bowl of Vesta beef risotto, and I learned how she had gone electronic. Her radiogram had suddenly blown a crystal, which meant no World Service. She had rushed to the shops with her bank book to find an alternative, and seen an advert for a build-it-yourself CB radio. She bought it, and the cheapest pocket transistor to keep her going. It was an extravagance, but the Society had just collapsed, and she needed something to take her mind off it. She said it was very difficult, but she'd done it, just the same, and now she regularly spoke to Christians all over England, as well as listening to the radio. Already, there were plans of a meeting, and a newsletter for electronic believers.

'It's the Lord's will,' she said, 'so don't pester me when I'm doing it.'

Perhaps it was the snow, or the food, or the impossibility of my life that made me hope to go to bed and wake up with the past intact. I seemed to have run in a great circle, and met myself again on the starting line.

Sir Perceval stayed on his narrow chair long after his host had left for sleep. Under the burning torch he puzzled over his hands. One hand was curious, sure and firm. His gentle, thoughtful hand. The hand for feeding a dog or strangling a demon. The other hand looked underfed. A stark, questioning, blank, un-comfortable hand. A scared hand but the hand for balancing. Perceval had been angry that night. His journey seemed fruitless, and himself misguided. His host had asked him why he had left, not really wanting to hear, presuming reasons of his own, that the king was mad, or the Round Table ruined. Perceval had stayed silent. He had gone for his own sake, nothing more. He had thought that day of returning. He felt himself being pulled like a bobbin of cotton, so that he was dizzy and wanted to give in to the pull and wake up round familiar things. When he slept that night he dreamed he was a spider hanging a long way down a huge oak. Then a raven came and flew through his thread, so that he dropped to the ground and scuttled away.

When I woke the next day, the sun was just forcing itself through the snow clouds, against the dusty window. The house felt quiet. Usually, my mother played tapes, and I could hear her singing along, or working out a new harmony. She had started to travel with Pastor Finch and his demon bus, whenever he came to the area. She felt she'd had a lot of experi-ence and would be a help to other distressed parents with demon-possessed children. She'd begun a self-help kit for the spiritually disturbed. What not to do, who to contact, which passages of the Bible to read. And of course, the choir liked to make tapes, to sing the demon away. Most were Pastor Finch's own compositions. I was glad she had a hobby, but not pleased that my particular sins were listed in the self-help kit. Still, at least she hadn't stuck in a passport photograph, warning the North-West to lock up their daughters.

I stayed with them until just after Christmas. Forced to watch endless programmes on the Nativity, and to eat mince pies with Mrs White, who was so nervous she started to hiccough uncontrollably.

'Jack, get the smelling salts,' ordered my mother, seizing Mrs White's nose till she went blue. The smelling salts didn't work, and Mrs White had to be taken to the bus stop on my father's arm.

'It's all your fault,' grumbled my mother. 'And on Christmas Eve too.' Then she went back into the living room to take a sip of port and peek at the Christmas presents. She couldn't bear not to open her presents, and it was still only eleven o'clock.

We decided to play Beetle to pass the time.

'You've cheated,' exclaimed my mother, as I fitted the last red leg on my insect. 'Never trust a sinner.'

'All right, we'll play again.' And we did, right up until five minutes to twelve, when my mother leapt up and switched on the radio to hear Big Ben. 'Get your glass,' she cried, filling it up with lemonade and a smattering of port. 'Merry Christmas, praise the Lord, now what have I got?' And she made a dive for her pile under the tree.

'Look, you've pulled the angel down,' I complained. She stuffed it back upside-down, one hand still tearing off the paper.

'This is from Pastor Spratt,' she said eagerly. I nodded, wondering what on earth could be that shape and get through customs.

'Oh look,' she cried.

It was an elephant's foot, with a hinged top. She hesitated a moment, then flung back the lid. It was an elephant's foot Promise Box; two layers of little scrolls, all rolled up, each with a promise from the Word. My mother had tears in her eyes, as she put it carefully on top of the sideboard.

'What's this from Auntie Maud?' I asked, picking out a hard, long object.

'Oh it'll probably be a sword stick, you know what she's like.' My mother tapped her head. 'It's this I'm interested in, from your father.'

It was flat, and not very well wrapped. Slowly she unravelled it, and there it was, a catapult. I couldn't believe it.

'Why's Dad bought you a catapult?'

'I asked him to, it's to get rid of them cats next door.' And she told me how she'd tried everything from scraps to menaces. But still they peed on her prize roses. She was going to ping at them now with dried peas. I shook my head, not knowing how to say that I had only bought her a cardigan . . .

I didn't see much of them for the next couple of days; they were at church. And it was in the first post after Christmas that my mother received the dreadful news. It was about the Morecambe guest house again, or rather, its owner Mrs Butler.

'Definitely a job for Pastor Finch,' said my mother, putting on her coat to go to the phone box. As soon as she had gone I picked up the letter. It seemed that Mrs Butler, depressed by falling numbers at the guest house, and frustrated by the constant nagging of the health authority, had taken to drink. More importantly, she had got herself a job as matron of a local old folk's home. While there she had taken up with a strange charismatic man who had once been the official exorcist to the Bishop of Bermuda. He had been dismissed under mysterious circumstances for some kind of unmentionable offence with the curate's wife. Back in England and safe within the besotted arms of Mrs Butler, he had persuaded her to let him practise voodoo on some of the more senile patients. They had been caught by a night nurse.

Imagine my mother's feelings; the Society for the Lost had been a bitter blow, the Morecambe guest house a terrible shock, but this was the final straw. I stared into the fire waiting for her to come home. Families, real ones, are chairs and tables and the right number of cups, but I had no means of joining one, and no means of dismissing my own; she had tied a thread around my button, to tug when she pleased. I knew a woman in another place. Perhaps she would save me. But what if she were asleep? What if she sleepwalked beside me and I never knew? Then the back door slammed and my mother marched in on a gust of wind, the knot of her head-scarf blown up on to her cheek like a patterned goitre. 'What a mess,' she raged, throwing the letter on to the fire. 'If I'm not sharp I'm going to miss my broadcast. Fetch the headphones.' I passed them over to her, and she adjusted the microphone.

'This is Kindly Light calling Manchester, come in Manchester, this is Kindly Light.'